Full Circle

Philip D. Bliss

Fulcrum Publishing

ISBN Paperback: 978-1-959616-09-2

ISBN Hardback: 978-1-959616-11-5

ISBN eBook: 978-1-959616-10-8

Author's Notes

Wait, this is not the title that was promised at the end of Unraveled. No, it is not, but after some prayer and searching my imagination, I decided to make Jake go full circle. You'll have to read on to find out what that means. This is the last book in the series, at least for now. I intend it to be, but if God should tell me to write another, I am sure I will. This book tackles many tough questions, but probably the most contemporary one, at least at the time of this writing, is the mystery behind AI. I won't spoil the book, but I invite you to read the afterword once the book is complete.

I wanted to incorporate my love of science-fiction into this book, but also keep it contemporary as well. So, that gave way to a new character that very well may show up in some other books as well. The names may change, but I can see this type of character appearing again.

I do hope you have enjoyed reading this series as much as I have enjoyed writing it. My goal all along has been to teach many aspects of a relationship with God. I have grown closer to Him through writing over the last five years, and I hope all of you who have traveled with Jake have been able to deepen your relationship with God as well. To quote Jake Anderson, "A relationship with God is the best thing He has given us, apart from the gift of eternal life through the sacrifice of His Son."

Enjoy book four of the Pop-Up Pastor series.

Dedicated to all of the readers of the Pop-Up Pastor Series. You have inspired me to keep writing. This book is for you.

Chapter One

And So It Begins...Again.

B raised short rib, tomato soup, and a pickle spear. A beautiful meal sat in front of me as I gazed out the window at the black silo marking my location: The Creamery – Beaver, Utah. The big white cow beneath the name struck me as a clever, professional detail. I realized I'd forgotten to ask for wheat bread, but the sourdough slices looked inviting, serving as sturdy hosts for the beefy delight on my plate. I picked up the pickle and moved it aside, knowing I had no plans to eat it. I reached for the sandwich, then hesitated and set it back down. My eyes found the black silo again. My mind drifted into that odd space where you're awake but not really thinking, almost motionless. The sounds around me faded into a dull hum as I remained absorbed in my thoughts.

Is this what I really want? Will it do any good?

I waited for a reply from God but heard nothing. His still-silent voice did not speak, yet I felt the strength and peace of His presence.

This is not about me. It's about Barry.

"Is everything okay, sir?"

I snapped back to reality. "Oh yes, I am still trying to decide if I am hungry or not. It's not the food, I assure you."

"Ok, well, let me know if you need anything."

The waitress was young—probably in her twenties. In many ways, she reminded me of Charlotte. Her smile could intoxicate the unsuspecting, and her calm voice quieted the anxiety I felt. I glanced again at the sandwich, lifted it, and took a bite. Mmm. *This is good.* My mind stayed alert, but the surrounding noise faded into silence as my thoughts began to drift. I didn't notice footsteps approaching, nor did my gaze cue my brain that someone was standing before me.

"Jake? Jake Anderson?"

I looked up. I didn't recognize the man. I searched my mental rolodex, trying to place his familiar face. He must have picked up on my confusion. I swallowed, clearing my mouth. "I'm not from around here."

"Yes! Maryland, right? Or am I mistaken? You look just like Jake Anderson, from Maryland."

Now my attention sharpened, and I mentally sorted through images faster. The connection clicked, and my voice responded. "You work for Davidson Ford? I bought my car there a few years back." I struggled to remember his name, and finally it surfaced—*Ray Davidson, Saul's son.*

"Yes, you do remember me." He gestured toward the empty seat across from me. "May I?"

"Of course, please sit. Can I get you something to drink? I'll call the waitress over."

"No, I'm just here to pick up a takeout order, but I saw you and thought it might be you. I think it's been..." He glanced outside as he searched his memory. "Four years?"

"I think that's right. Wow, I can't believe it's been that long. How's your dad? Is he well?"

He shifted in the booth, looking down at his folded hands. "Thanks for asking, Jake." He locked eyes with me. "He passed away about two months ago. Just didn't wake up one morning."

As a pastor, I never grew numb to hearing the news of someone's passing, but this felt different. I'd only had one conversation with Saul Davidson, yet he'd shaped my journey across the country on Interstate Seventy. Having lost both my parents, I empathized with the loss the young man felt. No matter our parents' age, losing them is difficult, and two months is never enough time to recover. I felt his pain. "I'm so sorry. It's never easy to lose your dad."

"Thanks, Jake. He was a wonderful man and touched many lives, but now he's with our Lord, and he's at peace. Yesterday was tough—it was the first Father's Day without him—but my wife and kids took me out to eat, so it was all good."

"Yes, it isn't quite the same once you lose your dad." I didn't let it show, but I had forgotten that yesterday was Father's Day. Charlotte never called me.

"I don't mean to pry, but I'm surprised to see you in Beaver again. Are you making another trip across the states on seventy?"

I saw genuine curiosity in his expression, but I also knew this change of subject eased the pain of talking about his father's death. I pushed my food tray to the right. *I'll get a box for it.* "Um, no, I'm headed to Cedar Valley to..."

"Cedar City?"

"Sorry?"

"You said Cedar Valley. Did you mean Cedar City? It's about forty minutes from here. Are you going to the Shakespeare Festival? Wait, let me guess—*Something Rotten*?"

"Sorry, what? No... I just wasn't very hungry." I looked at my cold platter.

He shook his head. "No, not the food. The braised short rib here is phenomenal. I meant, are you going to see *Something Rotten*? Tonight's the opening night at the Jones Theatre. I have tickets for this weekend. My wife and I are driving down on Friday and will spend the night in Cedar City."

I nodded. I didn't know Cedar City had a Shakespeare Festival, and as I thought about it, I couldn't recall a play called *Something Rotten*. It sounded more like a Dr. Seuss title to me. "I'm not familiar with the festival. Is it new? Well known?"

"Oh, it's definitely known in Utah. Not sure about Maryland. It's been around since 1961; they're a nonprofit that puts on plays every year from June to October."

"Wow, that's a long festival."

"Well, it's not really a festival. It's more like a..."

"Would you like to order something, JJ?" The waitress seemed to know him. *JJ? Must be a nickname.*

"Oh, hi, Marissa. I actually have a takeout order. It should be ready now."

"I'll check for you. Want me to take that plate, sir?" Marissa, the waitress, pointed to my barely eaten sandwich tray.

"No, actually," I pulled it closer. "Can I get a box to go?"

"Absolutely."

"Where was I?" He squinted. "Oh yes..." The sudden flash of white around his eyes made me open mine wider, too. "I was telling you about the Shakespeare Festival. They're a nonprofit company, not an actual festival. I know, funny name, but they do a lot for the community and the college."

"College?"

He paused, and the surprise on his face made me sit back a little. "Oh, right—you're not from around here. Southern Utah University is in Cedar City, and many of the festival's plays are performed in their theaters."

I watched his gaze drift beyond me, lips pressed together. He looked like Pavlov's dog. I was right; Marissa returned with a small bag and a paper cup with a plastic lid.

"Here's your order." She handed him the items and set a box on the edge of my table before walking away.

"Thank you, I'll leave a tip here on the table." He turned back to me. "She's the best. Great waitress. So, yeah, the festival is a must-see. But I interrupted—you were saying why you're here."

My sandwich was still warm as I placed it in the box. Deep down, I knew it might end up in the trash before I ate it. I didn't feel hungry. "Well, I flew into Grand Junction yesterday morning to meet someone. Then when I woke up this morning..."

"From Maryland?"

His interruption caught me off guard. "Um, no, I had to stop in Dallas."

"Yeah, DFW would have been my guess. GJT doesn't have many direct flights, but Dallas is a popular hub."

This didn't seem like the Ray Davidson I remembered from four years ago. "Anyway, I'm going to see a man in Cedar Va... City. Cedar City. Have you ever heard of Barry Goldberg?"

"Oh, sure. Who hasn't heard of the successful movie producer and local philanthropist? You know, he once gave $100,000 to Southern Utah University and didn't even ask for his name on a building. Who does that?"

His excitement made me lean back. "Anyway, I told you about my wife, Jane, right?"

"Yes, I remember you mentioning her. So tragic."

"Anyway, Jane has a sister who's a traveling nurse. She's currently caring for Mr. Goldberg at his home in Cedar..."

"Oh, I hadn't heard he wasn't well."

Another interruption. I watched as he closed the Styrofoam lid. I looked him in the eye. "Mr. Goldberg asked Jennifer if she knew..."

"Who's Jennifer?"

I wanted to yell, *Really, dude?* But kept my emotions in check. "Jennifer is Jane's sister." I paused, expecting another intrusion. "Jennifer called me and said Mr. Goldberg wants to speak with the—quote—'smartest Christian man she knows.' So, I agreed to meet with him. Plus, I wanted to check on Charlotte, but she hasn't...'"

"Charlotte?"

His tilted head made it clear he didn't know who I meant. My meeting with him and his father happened at the start of my trip. I guess he hadn't read my book, not that he should. "Yeah, it's a long story, but Charlotte is a girl I met during my last trip. We developed a relationship." When his mouth opened, I pressed on. "Not that kind of relationship. More of a father-daughter thing. Again, long story."

"No worries. Well, it was good to see you. I should get back to the dealership. Stop by if you have time; I'm sure the guys would like to see you. We remodeled and expanded, too." He leaned away from the table as he stood. "Oh, do you still have that Fiesta? I could give you a great deal on a Bronco or Escape."

"No, thanks. I traded the Fiesta for a Sierra 1500 a while back."

"What?" I smiled as several heads turned toward the outburst. "You didn't get an F-150?"

I felt a brief moment of judgment, as if I were worse than Benedict Arnold. "I wanted a black truck, got a good deal. Sorry if I offended."

"No worries, friend. All in jest. Take care, and if you get a chance, catch a show. I recommend *Something Rotten* or *Twelfth Night.* If you want to see *Twelfth Night* with my wife and me on Friday, look me up." He made a finger-gun gesture, winked his left eye, and clicked his tongue. "Catch you later, gator."

If this is how this trip is going to go, I might catch a flight back to Grand Junction. The thought quickly passed as Marissa reappeared at my table, and I thanked her for her service. I left a twenty-dollar bill on the table—for my food and the tip Ray either forgot to leave or never intended to leave. I couldn't decide which. As I walked to my rental car, a sudden realization struck me. I walked back inside. The timing was perfect—Marissa was heading toward me.

"Excuse me, ma'am, the man who sat with me—was his name Ray Davidson? Do you know?"

She laughed. "That wasn't Ray—that was Jim Johnson, but we all call him JJ. I'm surprised he actually let you talk. He works with Ray at the dealership."

I smiled. The irony wasn't lost on me. JJ had mentioned *Twelfth Night*, and I'd chatted with him all the while mistaking his identity. I couldn't help but laugh. "Well, he interrupted a lot."

"Yeah, he's known for that."

"Thank you, ma'am. You were wonderful today. May you have a blessed day."

I kept laughing. I had recognized him as someone from the car dealership, but it wasn't Ray Davidson—it was Jim, the guy who had interrupted me constantly. He loved sharing facts and tried to tell me all about Cove Fort and what my dream might have meant. Four years earlier, my wife and son had passed in a tragic car accident. After a few weeks, I had a dream about Cove Fort, Utah, and my home state of Maryland, and Interstate Seventy, which connects the two states. I discerned that God wanted me to travel across the country for forty days on Interstate Seventy. I eventually wrote a book about my journey of faith and healing.

I had stopped at a dealership in Beaver, where I purchased the car I used to travel the highway. While I was there to buy the vehicle, JJ kept interrupting me as I tried to explain why I bought a car in Utah, even though I live in Maryland. *I guess some things never change.* As I started the rental, I wondered to myself: *if that wasn't Ray, then is Saul still alive?*

"Hey Siri."

"Mm-hmm."

"Search for obituaries for…" I stopped.

"Who do you want to search for?"

"Cancel."

"Okay."

I didn't want to know. My intentions at that moment didn't feel right. Instead, I offered a prayer for Jim, Ray, and Saul. I felt a strong temptation to stop at Davidson Ford, but it would have meant going out of my way. It didn't matter—I knew I needed to rely on God, His grace and love, and not try to predict the future from a prophet. *That's divination, Jake.* I continued my journey, wondering about the man I was about to meet. *What Jewish man wants to debate a Christian?* I knew I'd find out soon enough. Until then, patience.

I glanced at my rental car's clock. My previously announced arrival time closely matched the GPS estimate. "Well, here goes nothing. It's in your hands, God. May I serve You well!"

The afternoon sun created a mirage of steamy waves on the blacktop as I drove. I let go of thoughts about intentions and focused on the Lord. I prayed silently as contemporary Christian music played from my phone through the car speakers. The miles passed quickly, and my sense of time felt short. Forty minutes later—and after a near miss with an armadillo crossing the road—I arrived at my destination. I said a prayer, thanking God for the opportunity before me, and asked Him to guide my new encounter. I prayed it would be a good distraction from the news I'd heard earlier that day.

Chapter Two

Big House! Big Ideas?

As the paved driveway cleared the trees, I gasped at the beauty of the home. It was long and tall. I could see at least three stories. On the left side, only the second and third floors had windows, with a small row of basement-style panes near the ground, while the right side featured them across all three levels. The architecture looked historic, and the roof shone of brown metal, probably a later upgrade. The outside walls were made of stone. Unless upgraded, it probably had lime mortar holding it all together. A large, welcoming black door stood in the middle, with a long, chained chandelier, like that of the White House, separating the two sides of the building.

I could not help but think of the famous, often misunderstood passage in John 14. "My Father's house has many rooms; if that were not so, would I have told you that I am going there to prepare a place for you?" Many believe this passage means we will all have mansions in heaven, but few grasp the pride that accompanies that thought. Jesus never meant to tell us we would have a mansion. In fact, the Greek word mone, often translated as "mansion," is better rendered as "dwelling" or "abode." It's not the mansion many think Jesus promised. But beyond that, Jesus meant a spiritual dwelling with God.

The belief that we have a mansion is very satisfying to the flesh, especially when someone lives on Earth in a small or humble home or apartment. The excitement of living in a mansion is very appealing to those who do not have one. But Jesus and the Father both intend that our spirit dwell amid the Father's spirit. That's why the Holy Spirit dwells in the hearts of believers. It's a preparation for dwelling with God forever.

The house before me could easily be considered a mansion. Some early-1800s Southern plantation homes featured a basement and a sub-basement, as well as three to four floors, housing many families, enslaved people, and distinguished guests. This home modeled that design—all-white with dark-gray, carefully curated and designed shutters adorned each window. The driveway circled and looped back upon itself, but an extension veered to the left. I assumed it led to a multiple-car garage behind the structure. Sculpted hedges lined the twenty-foot-long and ten-foot-wide marble sidewalk leading to the inviting double wood door structure. It almost seemed out of place in Utah, where much of the state is dry, and it costs money to maintain a lawn like this home had. The wooden structure didn't match the typical adobe-style dwellings found in the Southwest.

As I parked the car, two men exited the structure. One, wearing a formal black suit, stood by the door, waiting, while the other walked to my side of the vehicle.

"Welcome, Mr. Anderson. I am Gene. I would be happy to park your car in our garage. The Butler will welcome you and take you to your room."

Gene was tall, about my height, but weighed much less. My mom used to call people like him lanky. He wore a blue coverall that displayed his name on the left side. It had flecks of gray paint speckled all over it. I stepped out and handed him the key fob. A sharp tone rang through the air as I removed the key from the vehicle. Gene took the key ring from me, and when he sat down, the tone silenced. "Thank you, Gene." I started to reach for a ten-dollar bill I had left over from my lunch, but he pulled away before I could offer it to him. *I hope he will grab my bag.*

The smell of fresh flowers filled the air, and I saw a hint of red and yellow beyond the shrub-lined sidewalk. I traversed the three steps to the massive porch where two rockers adorned the edges. It reminded me of the rockers at Davidson Ford, where I sat and talked with Saul. James extended his hand, and I followed his pattern.

"I am James, the butler of the home, and I will escort you to your room. Gene will ensure your luggage and any other belongings are waiting for you in your room upon arrival. First, let me show you around. There are some public rooms and various restricted rooms. It is best you know right away where you are permitted and where you are not."

James was much shorter than Gene, I guessed five feet seven. He was what my mom would have called squatty. I never understood the meaning of her terms, but I came to know what each meant. He had a beard with gray lines running through it. Beneath his jacket, I saw tzitzits, a common Jewish custom. The tzitzits were worn on the corners of their garments, so when they looked upon them, they would remember to keep the commandments of God. The command to wear them came first in Numbers 15, and Moses reiterated it in Deuteronomy 12. *No mistake about it — undeniably Jewish.*

We stepped inside, and I felt like I had entered a familiar scene from a movie. Before me, a staircase extended on both sides to a central point on the second floor. Red carpet lay upon the mahogany steps. Balusters that looked like pure gold guided one as they stood beneath a polished white rail. To my left, white French doors with curtains gathered in the center of each door showed a glimpse of a baby grand piano in the room beyond. The room seemed too small for what I saw from outside. To the right, an open doorway led to what appeared to be a dining room. The table, I am certain, cost more than the rental car I arrived in. Beyond either side of the staircase, a closed door with fancy designs across the middle and on the sides remained closed. *I could spend hours exploring here. It's definitely been upgraded with modern design and materials.*

"This is the main foyer; the room to the left is the music room. If you don't play piano, please do not enter. To the right lies the main dining room, where most of your meals await you. Please be on time for meals. Would you prefer the elevator or are you comfortable with stairs, sir?"

"Stairs are fine, but I am...."

James began walking toward the steps. He chose the left side. I followed behind, all the while taking in the artistry of the crystal chandelier that brightened the entire foyer. I looked up to see the ceiling. *Fifty, sixty feet? Maybe more?*

James recognized my amazement. "Our ceilings are forty-five feet in this area. We have three floors of living space and two basements. The home was built in 1890, and Mr. Goldberg purchased it in 2001 and has lived here ever since. Renovations for appearance upgrades occurred three years ago, and more are scheduled for two years from now, provided Mr. Goldberg still owns the home then. Are you familiar with Mr. Goldberg's source of wealth?"

I didn't know why it mattered. I didn't know why anything in this home mattered. I wondered whether the home gave way to pride or served as a means of avoiding taxes. Did he purchase the house and improve it as an investment, or did vanity of vanities run through his veins? "I believe he was a movie producer, right?"

"Is!" He quickly corrected me. "As well as a director, actor, and writer. Mr. Goldberg is a man of great talent."

We reached the top of the stairs, and James used a key to unlock a pair of French doors to the left, similar to the one on the first floor. "Please remain here a moment, sir."

Great talent? I had no doubts about his talent or his ability to make money. In my research on him after Jennifer asked me to visit, I learned that, as an heir to a wealthy family, Barry had invested his inheritance wisely, and his money had come not from his movie-making talent alone, but from sound investments in commodities and financial stocks. Before his diagnosis of non-Hodgkin's lymphoma, he had served for 15 years as the chairman of one of the largest banks in the United States, according to the website I had viewed. However, its accuracy could not be verified. *I should have dug deeper into his past.*

I tried to peek through the doors as James stepped through. I saw someone approach and recognized her as our eyes connected. Jane's older sister walked through the entrance and greeted me as James shut the door behind her. I recognized a click as the lock engaged. "Great to see you again," we embraced, and she squeezed tight.

"I am so happy you came. I am sorry I couldn't provide more details, but Mr. Goldberg insisted on doing it this way. Please, let's sit for a moment. Did you check out that website I sent you?"

I had not noticed the wingback chairs against the wall. She sat on the left and I on the right. A lovely fern centerpiece adorned the small table between us. I waited for her to speak, but she apparently had the same intention.

"I did get a chance to view it." The silence that ensued felt eerily uncomfortable.

"I..."

"Go ahead," I said as she smiled at our simultaneous interaction.

"I want to give you the details now. I am sure you have wondered why I asked you to come. I didn't think you would actually do it, but I'm glad you did. Mr. Goldberg is a man with big ideas."

I looked around at my surroundings. "A big house too."

She smiled. "Yes indeed. There are parts of this home I have never seen. I doubt you will either. Anyway, as you know, I have been serving as his nurse for three months now. In that time, he has shown great curiosity about my faith. He has asked me questions that I wasn't sure how to answer. I mean, I know why I believe, but I couldn't answer his questions about how Jesus ties to the Jewish faith. Mr. Goldberg has spent his entire life studying Judaism, and I think he has been taught that Christians are liars and thieves. He constantly says the book of Revelation is a stolen book."

I heard the argument many times. The illustrations in Daniel, Zechariah, Ezekiel, Joel, and Isaiah, as well as the symbolism of the Exodus, have led many in the Jewish faith to believe that Revelation was deliberately written to disparage or even mock the Jewish people. I have always seen it as confirmation and intelligent design. "I have heard that too. So, did he ask you to have me come so I can teach him about Revelation?"

She turned toward the French door and back to me. She leaned in and whispered. "The butler is almost certainly listening." She sat upright again and spoke in a normal voice. "Mr. Goldberg wishes to engage in a debate with a Christian before his passing, aiming to argue that Judaism is the only true faith and that Christianity is a cult. I was instructed not to share this information with the person I select until that individual arrives."

"Okay, I understand." I also leaned in to whisper. "I still would have come if I had known," we smiled as I sat up again. "Well, I would be glad to debate with him. Is there a format he wants to use? I mean, will there be a moderator and judges, or is it just one-on-one talks with him over a period of days? What's the plan? Do you know?"

"From my understanding...." She again looked toward the doors. "You will be called in at times during your stay. I hope you are okay with this, but even if you need to be woken up at night, he will expect you to come then and answer his questions. If you are outside getting exercise, you must come in when someone comes for you or when Emma calls. When he is done talking for the day, even if it has been ten minutes, you will be asked to leave and return to your room."

Emma? Who is Emma? "So, I am at his beck and call?"

"Well, that is one way to say it, I guess." The French door opened, and James appeared from the opposite side.

"Excuse me, Jennifer. Mr. Goldberg would like some water."

"Right away. Can I first finish what I was saying to..."

"Now, ma'am."

Jennifer grimaced and walked toward the double door before disappearing behind it. James locked the door, came toward me, and sat down. "Mr. Goldberg is not a man of 'beck and call', sir. He is a man of great importance, and you would do well, should you accept this honor to serve him, to see it as a great reward to be in his presence, let alone answer his questions when he asks. Sir, if you are not ready for the honorable challenge, I will see to it that your expenses are paid and that you are escorted to your car. " He grabbed a small walkie-talkie from his pocket. "Gene, are you around?"

"Go ahead for Gene."

"Mr. Anderson will be..." he unkeyed the mic. "Are you accepting or are you denying?"

"Well, I don't know for certain what I am accepting. Can I get some more details?"

"Accepting or leaving, sir, I need to respond to Gene."

I heard His voice clearly. The subtle, quiet, and gentle thought that appeared in my mind. *I want Baron.* "Is Mr. Goldberg's name Baron?"

With a disgusted gesture, James stood up. "Anyone can do a Google search to find that information. But yes. Now, I must assume you are declining the offer since you won't answer. Gene, Mr. Anderson is..."

"Staying!" I said loudly.

James looked at me with a smile. "Is staying Gene. Are his belongings in his room?"

"Yes, sir, and his car is in garage three and secured. Please tell Mr. Anderson to ring me if he needs his car. He can use the yellow phone or just speak to..."

"Thank you, Gene. Dismissed."

James walked past me to another set of doors. He turned the handle and opened the unlocked door. "Your room is this way, sir. A full set of rules and guidelines for your stay will be on the study table in your suite. I suggest you read it straight away, given the nature of certain items that some have had problems with in the past. The temperature has been adjusted to the current weather, and your clothing has been put in the wardrobe. Linens and bed sheets will be changed weekly on Sundays according to the schedule posted on the study table. A laptop with high-speed internet access is available for your research. Meals will be served in the main dining room that you saw when you walked in. If you are not seated at the scheduled time, it will be assumed that you are not hungry. You may have two hours of recreation twice a day at the appropriate time..."

I stopped listening. I guessed his next words would be '*follow the schedule,*' and indeed, he spoke in turn. James continued to drone as we walked the long corridor. Some rooms had numbers, and some had symbols. I saw a tree, a cat, and a seal among other unrecognizable features. Walking past one room, I distinctly smelled chlorine, and James confirmed it as the natatorium. We walked for what seemed almost a minute, and he stopped at a door at the edge of the hallway.

"This is your suite. It's a corner room, and I hope you will find it accommodating. There will be a spiral staircase that intersects your floor. You cannot go up as there is a locked door at the landing on the third floor, but you are permitted to travel down, which will lead you to a private entrance connected to the east garden. Please enjoy some recreation time according to the daily schedule. If you continue to the first basement, you will find a welcoming selection of wine. You may partake as you wish. Please know that this room is locked from the outside. You can enter this wine cellar, but you must have a key to exit, and no key has been provided. So, I suggest you don't lock yourself in. The guidelines will teach you what to do in such a situation. You cannot enter the sub-basement from this level, nor at all. It is for storage and maintenance personnel only. If you need assistance with anything, use the yellow phone. If you have an emergency, pick up the red phone, and someone will assist you. Are there any questions?"

"Yeah, it seems you don't want me to go in that wine cellar, right?"

"You are free to go in, sir, but you will almost assuredly be locked in. So the choice is yours. Any other inquiries?"

I shook my head. The truth is, many questions filled my mind, but I had hoped to ask them when alone with Jennifer. Seeing that door locked behind her concerned me. *Are we prisoners here? Did I enter the Hotel California?* I laughed at the thought. The song started playing in my mind.

"There is no key for your room. It is a four-digit code: your birthday, month, and day. We have found that to be the easiest for guests to remember."

"Thank you, James. Can I offer you a tip?" I pulled a twenty out of my front pocket.

"I am well paid, sir; I do not need your charity." He walked away as I entered my room.

Room? The term did not apply. Apartment seemed more appropriate. But he called it a suite. *I guess that does fit.* I noticed my suitcase had been placed in a small opening with a shelf above it, holding a blanket and a pillow—a closet without a door. A large sofa situated in front of a large flat screen television sat before me. To the left, I could see a door leading to a queen-sized bed. To the right in the room, I saw another door. Presumably the bathroom. To my right, a small kitchen area with a refrigerator and stove. *Yeah, more like a studio apartment.* I had never seen anything like it and probably never would again. I checked my watch. I had been awake for seventeen hours, and that was only after sleeping for three. I walked toward the bedroom, closed the door behind me, and lay down for a much-needed nap. I hoped to catch up with Jennifer at some point, and the wine cellar offered great curiosity as well. I felt the bed's soft comfort and fell asleep within minutes.

Chapter Three

The Test

The dark hallway floorboards creaked as I walked. My hand lightly touched the wall to steady my sense of direction. I hoped to see even a shred of light beneath any of the doors, but none existed. I stopped and listened intently. I thought I heard creaking behind me. I craned my neck and turned slightly to the left. I could not see anything.

"Someone there?"

No reply. I waited until the silence gave way to ringing in my ears again, and I stepped forward. Two steps, and I heard the creaking again. As a child, I feared the dark and alligators under my bed. I thought I had overcome both fears, but this corridor's darkness penetrated my faith, and fear found a way into my soul. "Who's there?" I yelled, but my voice could not be heard this time. I tried to speak again, but nothing came out. Panic set in. *My voice is gone*. I tried to move, but I remained paralyzed. I tried to move my legs, but they seemed glued to the floor. I tried to lift my arms, but I could not feel them. I tried to turn toward the footsteps behind me. Slowly, I adjusted to my surroundings and saw Charlotte appear behind me, her hand on my head, pushing. I tried to scream, but nothing came.

"Mr. Anderson, your presence is requested at the stairwell."

The moment reality begins to set back in after awakening from a night-mare is both relieving and confusing. Seconds later, the fear left, and I realized I lay on the bed that I had lain upon forty minutes earlier for a nap.

"Mr. Anderson, will you please respond?"

I winked briskly and raised my left hand to rub my face. Fully conscious now, I responded, "I'm here." However, I did not know with whom I conversed. "Who's here?" I wasn't sure whether the words were the result of the dream or a keen sense of someone in my room. I rolled over to my back as the voice spoke again.

"Mr. Anderson, please return to the staircase. Do you confirm?"

I didn't recognize the female voice. "Yeah, I will be right there." I had not seen a speaker in the ceiling before. I still did not see it as I looked intently.

"Very well. Thank you."

I squinted, trying to determine where the microphone hid from my sight. *I don't like that Big Brother is watching.* I rolled to the edge of the bed and found my footing. *What did I get myself into?* I let the thought pass and moved to the door. I expected it to be locked, but it opened freely. Within a minute, I saw James standing near the wingback chairs, looking at his watch.

"Am I late?"

He didn't acknowledge my inquiry. "Follow me, please." He unlocked the double French door and walked through.

"Why is this door always locked?"

"For security reasons." I took it as a don't-ask, don't-tell situation. I knew there had to be more to it. "Mr. Goldberg would like to ask you two questions. How you answer will determine how we proceed. Was your nap good?"

I stopped briefly as he kept walking. "Were you watching me too?"

James turned to face me. "No, sir. We do not have cameras in the guest rooms. Mr. Goldberg is not a voyeur, and the microphone is only active when the speaker is on. It will only be used to request your presence. I take it you did not read the guidelines on the study table?" His left eyebrow raised. His inquisitive demeanor drove a dagger through me. I nodded and began walking again. He did the same. "It's for security reasons only. They are not always listening to voices. They pick up...They sense things." His demeanor changed. He hid something. "Like breath sounds, ok."

"Ok, I guess. I am not sure if I like that, but I will adjust. And who was the female voice?"

"Read the guidelines, please, Mr. Anderson. Now let's go."

The hallway resembled the one on the opposite side; however, there were fewer doors, and I did not smell chlorine. Rooms only appeared on the right side of the hall. No entrances on the left. No windows either. Curiosity ensued. "How many people live here?"

"Why does that matter to you?"

"Just curious."

"Good thing you are not a feline then, sir."

I understood the semantics but wondered whether he meant it symbolically or literally. *Indeed, the former.*

"If you must know, Mr. Goldberg bought this house for his wife, but she has passed. His son has never lived here and has not had contact with him for over twenty years. I live here, as does Gene. The main chef and the three-person cleaning staff live on the third floor. We used to employ more, but at the time, this is all there is. Oh, and Jennifer is a temporary resident, as you are too, sir. I know, however, that she has read the guidelines. The locks are for security. I have had death threats from people who do not consider me a friend." He paused outside a single door. The distance between the outside wall and the next door indicated it may be Barry's room. "Any further questions?"

I paused and looked around. "You have had death threats?"

"No, sir, I said Mr. Goldberg has received death threats."

"Well, I am pretty sure you said you."

"Believe what you want, the truth will always ring true. Do you have any other questions?"

Do you not like me? "No, I think I am good. Thank you, James."

"I understand this is an enormous house, but I assure you that Mr. Goldberg is quite the simple man."

Very simple, I'm sure. I nodded and looked down.

James opened the door and stepped in behind him. The smell of antiseptic reminded me of a hospital. The massive room seemed to go on forever, but in the middle of the marble floor, a hospital bed lay with a man I presumed to be Baron Goldberg upon it. Our eyes met, and I felt my soul being penetrated by a man who had been through many trials in his life. He looked toward Jennifer, who changed a saline bag beside his bed. She pushed a few buttons while he spoke softly to her. She turned to me, then back to him, and nodded. I didn't notice that James had stood by the door when Barry called me over with a waving motion of his right hand that remained free of tubes. A monitor beside the bed measured his vitals. Multiple-colored lines and numbers changed every second, and I heard a faint beep, which I assumed was calibrated to his heart rate.

"Mr. Anderson, I presume?"

I extended my hand, and he did as well. "Yes, Mr. Goldberg. It's a pleasure to meet you."

"Well, if Jennifer is correct, the pleasure is all mine."

I looked at Jennifer. She smiled again before returning to her work. Mr. Goldberg studied me. Eyes scanned me from top to bottom as he held onto my hand. He released me and looked at Jennifer.

"Do you know why I called you here, sir?"

"Jennifer started to fill me in, and James told me about a book of guidelines that I need to read still, but have…"

"Bah! he is too critical. Read the first page and forget the rest. It's the most important. I mean, if you want to use them to help you sleep, then by all means, read the rest. Did he also tell you that you can't go to certain rooms, especially the sub-basement?"

"Yes, he did, sir. I will be sure to obey..."

"Bah! Mi casa es su casa. ¿Sí entiendes?"

"I do actually know a little Spanish, sir, and yes, I understand. I will probably remain in my room. The accommodations are nice. I really appreciate your hospitality."

"Well, Mr. Anderson. Can I call you Jake?"

"Absolutely."

"Jake, I mean it. If you want to explore, you can. If anyone stops you, tell them that you are Barry's guest and that he said you could explore. I have a great staff. I am sure the butler will ease up, but please tell me if he doesn't."

"Ok, sir, thank you."

"He means it, Jake. Mr. Goldberg is a good man. The butler is..."

"Is a stiff," added Barry.

I tried not to laugh, but when Jennifer and Barry did, I let it out. I pegged James as the oldest child. Stereotypically, they tend to be rule followers, and he certainly seemed like a rule follower. "May I sit?"

Barry nodded. "Please do." He coughed violently, and alarms started with higher tones. Jennifer did not seem to be concerned. Moments later, he settled, and the alarms did too. "Jake, are you a Christian man?"

Was that the first question? "Yes, sir, I am."

"Good, I have two questions for you before we proceed. Just a small test to see who I am dealing with. Are you okay with that?"

That answers that question. "Sure, I will do my best to answer."

He shifted in his bed. "Can I be raised a little? You have already answered my main question. You recognized me when you walked in. I wanted to be sure you knew who I was."

Jennifer pushed a few buttons, and Barry's head leaned forward, and his bed raised. I looked at him, now eye level. *You know who I am? Is he arrogant much?* "To be quite honest, sir, I apologize as I don't watch many movies, but I only presumed you are Barry Goldberg since that is who Jennifer requested I visit. I assumed you were Mr. Goldberg, right?"

"Yes, you passed. Please don't take my last statement as arrogance. I do not expect to be known." He raised his hand and made air quotes. But I wanted to be sure you knew who you were dealing with. Now tell me, please." He winced, seemingly from pain, and grabbed his side. Jennifer observed. "What is Torah?" he strained out in a weak voice.

"What is Torah?" I thought for a moment and prayed for the correct answer. *The Law* seemed the proper response, but I knew that, as a Jewish man, he sought a different answer. Years ago, before Jane and I married, I met a man who taught me a great deal about Jewish culture and the Bible. He told me that Torah is not the law, but rather a teaching. "Well, it is the oral and written instruction given to the chosen people of God, the Hebrews, when they came out of Egypt. Moses received word-for-word these instructions and teachings during his forty-day conversation with God."

"Excellent, sir. I appreciate your mention of both oral and written. Very good. Next question. How do you understand the covenant that God made with the Hebrew people? Is this covenant still valid today?"

"I don't believe in replacement theology. I believe that God made a covenant with the people, under which He would bear the punishment if they broke it. Therefore, in a way, yes, I believe that Jesus did not nullify the original covenant, but rather He was the divine fulfillment of such a covenant for the people with which it was made."

He looked at Jennifer. "I was right to trust you. You were correct about him." Straining as he may, Barry turned toward me with a large grin painted upon his face. "Mr. Anderson, as you have been informed, I would like to debate with you, sir. I want to spend as much time as we can together in this room, the library across the hall, or perhaps in the garden on a cool day, as we discuss this man you know as your savior. At this moment, I still consider myself righteous through the covenant established with my people thousands of years ago. I have studied the Hebrew Tanakh my whole life, and one does not just toss it aside for a new belief. However, facing my own mortality has awoken me to a new possibility. I must consider why so many people believe in a man that my people crucified for being a false prophet and a blasphemer."

I weighed his comments thoughtfully before responding. I still did not know if this man sought to know the truth about Jesus or if he wanted to gain a notch in his belt before he passed from this life by showing a Christian how their beliefs did not stand up next to the long-standing tradition of Rabbis, the Talmud, and the deep theological thoughts of traditional Midrash. Praying once again in my mind, I asked God for the right words. I could tell he wanted a response from me. "Perhaps we can together help our broken world. We can partake in Tikkun Olam together, sir."

His eyes widened. He glanced at Jennifer, then at me. "Have you eaten anything, Jake? I have a feeling we could be in for a long night."

I started to answer when James walked in carrying a tray with a domed plate and a Styrofoam cup with a lid and a plastic straw protruding from the top. "Your dinner is ready, sir. Jake and Jennifer, if Mr. Goldberg approves, a meal has been prepared for you as well in the main dining room on the first floor."

"Yes, please, go eat you two. I will be ready for you when you return, Jake. What time is it?"

"It's 5:30 pm, sir.", James answered.

"Fantastic. Jake, if you please, I will expect to see you back at 7 pm. We will start with some basics. Do you agree, sir?"

James looked at me with intent after placing the tray he carried upon the side table next to the hospital bed. "Yes, if that is what you want, Mr. Gold..."

"It's Barry. I insist you call me Barry." James let out an audible scoff.

"Okay, Barry, I will be back at 7."

Jennifer walked around the bed, and together we made our way to the door.

"That will be all.", he spoke to James.

"But sir, I must address a crucial concern."

"That will be all." He spoke slowly and distinctly. I heard James walk behind us and huff slightly as he turned his back on Barry. I smiled as did Jennifer. I made a mental note to ask her for her opinion of James over dinner. I assumed we would eat together, but James may have other ideas.

***

While we sat at the table, Jennifer and I heard the female voice again. "Mr. Goldberg has decided to see you again in the morning. Enjoy your evening."

"Who is that?"

She laughed. "I guess you didn't read the guidelines."

"No, I haven't yet. I guess I need to."

"I recommend you do. It will explain a lot."

Dinner satisfied my hunger after the braised-rib lunch earlier that day—the *braised rib. Oh no, I forgot it.* "How can I get in contact with Gene?"

"He's right there," she pointed behind me, as Gene walked in. I didn't have a chance to ask him about the lunch I left in the back seat of my car. He anticipated my question.

"I put your doggie bag in the refrigerator in your room."

I smiled. It was all I could do. What started as a sad day for me earlier began to turn into an interesting one. I had no idea how rewarding it would eventually be. *I needed this distraction for sure.*

I could not be certain, and time would tell, but I thought I passed the first test with flying colors. My gut told me to leave, but my mind said stay and learn and teach. I chose to follow my mind instead of my gut this time. I finished my dinner but lacked the strength to talk. It had been a long day, and I needed to sleep off the jet lag.

I walked with Jennifer back to her room. She had a seal upon her door. I never thought to ask her what it represented. I then continued down the hall to the corner. Once inside, I tried to find the speaker and microphone again, but the ceilings were at least nine feet high, and I didn't see anything I could stand on. After saying some prayers, I lay down on the comfortable bed.

I had an eerie feeling I was being watched. After leaving the bed, I stood beneath what appeared to be a smoke detector. I stared at it for a few minutes, looking for lights or any resemblance to a speaker. I found none. Fatigue took over, and I lay back down. It didn't take long; I fell asleep for the night.

Chapter Four

Liquid Wisdom

S mokey sucked his tail until it became a glob of stiff fur. Snowball never liked being inside. Eight ball hid twenty-two hours of each day, and Buffy, Max, and Ricky were a trio of active personalities that lived long lives. I glanced at my phone on the nightstand: 1:35 A.M. As I lay thinking about the various cats I or my family owned during my lifetime, the one that sucked his tail remained the oddest, but it was the curiosity of Snowball I thought of at the moment. *Snowball would check out that wine cellar.* I couldn't decide if James purposely tempted me to visit the wine cellar beneath me or if he did mean to warn me not to go in. I have always liked a challenge.

As I approached the corner of the room, I moved the long white curtain, and, as James had indicated, a spiral staircase rose to the third floor and descended. I traversed down to a landing. A door, which led to the outside, showed the dim moonlight. I turned around, my iPhone flashlight lighting the wall. I saw no other doors. *Obviously, I am not permitted on the first floor.*

As I reached the next and final landing, the door appeared on the inside of the wall. I entered through it, but the area was dark. I touched both sides of the wall until I found a light switch. Several doors could be seen along the hall, but the door across from me was labeled "Liquid Wisdom". I laughed at the quip, but I knew I had found the right room. I wondered for a moment if James wanted me to see the clever title. But I decided it didn't fit his personality.

Temptation arose in my mind. I turned the handle, and it moved. I pushed, and the door opened. I waited for alarms or flashing lights, but saw none. I pushed a little more, and a light appeared in the room. It smelled musty and damp. I felt a slight temperature change as the air pressure between the two rooms balanced. I pulled it shut. *I shouldn't do this.* My hand remained on the handle. I took a deep breath, turned the handle, and pushed further this time.

Once inside the small seven-by-seven room, I noticed hundreds of bottles of wine in racks along the three walls I could see. All sense of what I had been told left me, and I let go of the door handle, which caused the hydraulic hinge to engage and the door shut behind me. The memory flooded my mind. 'It locks from the outside.' I turned, grabbed the handle, and tried to open, but indeed. I was locked in.

I rubbed my face as adrenaline raced through my body. My arms shook. I looked at the ceiling and saw only a small circular light. I tried the handle again, but it remained locked. Turning back, I thought I saw someone in the room. I blinked, and the figure disappeared. *Now, I am seeing things.*

"Okay, Jake, think."

I reached into my pockets. They were empty. I tried the handle a third time, but it still wouldn't budge. *I should have read those guidelines.* I turned in circles, looking for something that might assist my escape from the prison cell I had created for myself.

How long until someone realizes I am missing? Will they think to look here first? Should I yell? The questions raced fast. I could feel my heart pounding. I put my hand on my chest, and I physically felt the movement. I tried to calm my breathing. I had panic attacks in the past, but this one I caused myself.

After five minutes, I walked toward the door but stopped short of trying a fourth time to open it. I replayed the definition of insanity in my mind. I heard a faint beep.

"Data received." The voice sounded like Emma's, but it was much more mechanical.

I jumped at the sound of the female voice. I calmed my breathing and listened for more instructions. I heard nothing. It seemed like an hour, but another minute passed. I was now calm.

"Exercise complete."

I heard a click near the door handle. I reached for it and turned. I pulled the door toward me so fast I nearly hit my head with it. I jumped back as it swung open past me. The light shut off. I ran across the hall to the steps. The moon seemed to shine a little brighter as I passed the first level entrance. I prayed the door to my room would not be locked. As I arrived on the landing of the second floor, I remembered I didn't have a door. I saw light in my room, which I had not turned on, and I stepped in.

I grabbed my chest as it rose and fell with each labored breath. My first thought was to pack my clothes and leave, but a familiar female voice came over the hidden speaker.

"Mr. Anderson, would you like me to dim the lights for you?"

I didn't answer. I walked to the center of the room again, past the sofa. I looked up and saw a flashing red light in the smoke detector. I squinted as I tried to discern the device above me.

"Mr. Anderson, would you like me to dim the lights for you?"

"Yes", I said in a low whisper.

The lights went off. I bumped into the sofa as I ran for the bedroom. I jumped two feet from the bed and landed with a bounce. The blanket covered my fetal-style positioned body.

Was it a trap? Was it a game? Should I even mention it to anyone? As I processed each thought, I slowly fell asleep again.

Chapter Five

Lead By The Spirit

The wise older man spoke with intensity and creativity. He trusted his Savior and the gift of the Spirit that He promised. He paused his speech to find the right words. "Be respectful," he finally spoke. "Respect that the person you are speaking with has just as many interpretations about why you are wrong as you have about why you are right." I nodded in agreement. "Many Jews have suffered from unfathomable atrocities, and I am not even talking about the holocaust, though it was by far the worst. In times we only read about in history books, when we can no longer ask survivors what it was like, they suffered. Remember, the early Christians were still Jews who believed in Jesus as their savior, and they had families who suffered at the hands of the Romans." I continued to nod in agreement. "Remember how the Catholic church forced its way upon people who chose to associate with their institution and, forgive me for saying, changed the true understanding of being saved by grace through faith, and this not of yourselves. But I will also say this. They have probably done more for the poor than any other religious group in history. Praise God for their works."

"I understand what you mean. Respect is important for any conversation."

"The goal is not to debate or use proof texting. The goal is to respect, listen to, and honor their traditions and beliefs. Speak their language or, as Paul once said, 'Be all things to all people,' and not someone who feels they are doing the right thing by convincing all Jews to accept their messiah. You will never get very far if you take that approach, and that is why the church has failed its Jewish brethren over the years."

The conversation resonated in my mind. Twenty years earlier, at a campground near Massillon, Ohio, I spoke with a sage man of Jewish descent who had converted to what he called 'The Two-House Movement'. This concept, for all intents and purposes, is Christian. Still, they choose not to take the name Christian because it can carry a negative connotation among Jewish believers and non-believers alike. Yet a Jewish person who hears of the two-house movement will immediately identify with the Old Testament's House of Israel and the House of Judah. In particular, the major prophets. The man, whose name I could no longer remember, spoke prophetically over me that night, saying God had told him I would preach to the Jewish people and help them appreciate their messiah.

As I walked back to the room on the left wing of the home where I had met Barry Goldberg one day earlier, I replayed the words of that man in my mind. I also prayed God would prepare me for the encounter I was about to begin. *May Your Spirit guide me, Father.*

I entered the room and noticed Barry's closed eyes. I walked softly to the area his bed occupied. I had not seen it before, but the large room felt empty and dark, except for the bed and medical equipment surrounding him. A bright surgical light hung from the ceiling above him, but the remainder of the room remained dark. The steady beep of the monitors and the smell remained the same. All the corners seemed dark, and I wondered what might be in the shadows. I walked to the chair and looked beyond the equipment. The room's emptiness shocked me. Along the back wall, I saw a black curtain that extended from end to end. *I wonder what used to be here.*

Surely this was not created to be a hospital room only. I thought it seemed like a ballroom of some sort. The chair scuffed the floor as I pulled it toward me, and this awakened Barry.

"Jake, thank you for coming back. Would you mind raising my head? It's the blue button on the side rail."

As I stepped around the foot of the bed, I quickly recognized the symbol that signaled the head would lift. I pushed it until he motioned for me to stop. I wanted to ask him about my middle-of-the-night antics, but for now, I didn't bring it up.

"That's good. That's good. Now, where did we leave off?"

"Why don't we start with you telling me your story?" I asked as I walked back to the chair.

"Oh, you are good. I understand you are a pastor, no?"

"Yes, sir, I have a good deal of pastoral experience, and I have carried this title for a while. What gave it away?"

"A good pastor will always respect the person by asking for their story. It allows the sometimes anxious, untrusting, or nervous person to open up and connect with the person in front of them. Psychologically speaking, it is good practice for all of us, not just pastors."

"Well, I learned from a wise man years ago that when preparing to share with someone, it is always polite to allow that person to share their story."

"Indeed, it is Pastor Jake. That is why I insist that you go first. I especially would like to know why you believe what you believe. Trust me, it will go a long way with my next series of questions if I understand who you are. You impressed me with your knowledge of my faith, but I want to know about yours. I do not believe it alone will convince me to accept your messiah, but it will help me understand why you believe what you do."

I welcomed the question. In recent months, as Charlotte began to show signs of change, I turned to God, and He revealed to me countless reasons why I needed to understand myself and my faith. I moved from the 'I believe because I was told to' into a relational belief in my heavenly Father and His Son, who died for me. Barry's question was no coincidence, by any means. God knew I would need a stronger faith than I thought I had. He had prepared me for this event and started four years earlier with the death of my wife, Jane, and my son, Timmy.

The deep breath felt cleansing. "Where do I begin?" I did not know how much to share, nor what he already knew about me. I still did not know for sure what his goal in this debate was. *It's not a debate, it's a conversation. I don't owe him anything.* I decided that honesty was indeed the best policy. That teaching of my earthly father carried with me my whole life, and it certainly seemed appropriate at the present.

"Why not start at the beginning?" Barry asked.

"Yes, of course. Well, I never went to church much as a child. My earliest memory of being in a church was on a Sunday morning after spending the night with my grandparents. I don't even remember how old I was at the time. Maybe seven? I remember seeing men in trench coats and top hats, and the ladies in dresses, and some wore hats with netting and flowers in them."

"It sounds like you are describing a pillbox hat or maybe a fascinator."

Fascinator did not strike a chord with my memories, but I had heard the term pillbox hat. Perhaps he was right. "Yeah, that's maybe it. Anyway, I remember being told to be quiet. All I wanted to do was play, but I had to keep quiet. After grandma and grandpa sang a song, a man in a suit stood at the front and talked for what seemed like forever. I am sure he finished after twenty or maybe thirty minutes, but to a seven-year-old, that seemed like most of the day."

"Oh, your church traditions." He interpreted my eyes that squinted at him. "So sorry, sir. Please continue."

"No worries, Barry." I used his name to make our conversation personal. "After the man talked, everyone stood up. I distinctly remember them sitting on benches without backs. To me, it seemed they sat on baseball dugout benches. The men pushed them all toward the wall and began setting up tables. I could smell food, and the kitchen ladies began taking it out and setting it on the tables. But my grandparents grabbed me, and we left."

"Did you wear a suit?"

"Great question. I don't recall. But I probably did, because I knew it was winter, and the year before, on Christmas, I had opened a giant box. I expected some big toys, but I received a suit. My grandma called it a leisure suit. I had never heard of such a thing, but I distinctly remember being bummed that it wasn't a toy. To this day, I don't know the difference between a leisure suit and a regular suit." The laugh felt almost as good as the deep breath.

"A leisure suit? I remember when I was first given tzitzit. I bet I felt the way you did about the leisure suit. Do you know what a tzitzit is, Jake?"

"Yes, the tassels. Tied to the edge of your garment so that you can look upon them and remember to keep the commandments of God."

"You continue to impress. I have only met a handful of Christians who ever knew what they were called, and fewer knew why I wear them. Ok, so you went to church. What was next? Was this the only time you went as a child?"

"No, not at all. There was another time I went with my aunt and uncle for Easter. We were supposed to have an Easter Egg hunt after the service, and it rained all morning. I sat in a room." I paused to reflect. *Why was I not in the service?* "I guess the children were dismissed for junior church. I looked out the window and remembered asking God to make the rain stop so we could have our egg hunt."

"Did it stop?"

"It did. I was so thankful, and I thanked God for answering my prayer."

"He causes the wind to blow and the rain to fall."

"The Amidah?"

I noticed the heart rate on the monitor increased slightly. "Jennifer said you were a very learned man. She was correct. Yes, that is from the Amidah, or a prayer we speak often, if not daily. Once again, you continue to impress. Are you sure you are not what they call a messianic?"

That term sent reverberations through my soul. I had spent three and a half years in the Messianic movement, and it proved to be a time of growth but also a time of great consternation for me as well. "No, I am not part of the messy-antics movement."

He laughed heartily at my comment, "Oh, that's a good one I have not heard before. So, you mentioned Christmas and Easter. Are these the only times you went to church as a child?"

"Well, as far as I can remember, yes. I think I went about six times. At least that's what I always tell people, but I don't remember for certain."

"May I ask you. Did you feel God there? Or were you there because you were told?"

"Great Question!" I looked at the ceiling, a habit I often fall into when I want to think deeply. I could not remember a time when I did not feel God's presence. Even before I knew who God was, I knew there was someone unseen with me. When my dad told me about God, I said, 'Oh yeah, He is with me all the time.' My dad never forgot that moment and shared it with me often. I know many people go their whole lives without ever truly sensing or feeling God's presence. Unfortunately, for many, He remains only a concept—someone they believe in but do not truly experience. When that happens, they miss the more profound sense of His presence. Those who understand this, who know He is more than a concept, recognize that even when they do not consciously acknowledge Him, He is always with them. A relationship with God is the best thing He has given us, apart from the gift of eternal life through the sacrifice of

His Son. I looked Barry in the eyes. "I don't know a time I have not felt God."

"Interesting. We, Jews, know God is always with us, but someday I would like to comprehend this feeling of a personal relationship with Him. I have asked Him about it. I guess that's the first step. No?"

"Absolutely, that is a great first step. I tell people all the time to ask God to reveal Himself. Jeremiah 29:13″

"You will find me when you seek me with your whole heart," Barry added.

"A verse I live by, Barry."

"Is this the only exposure you had to your faith when you were young?"

"Oh no, not at all. My dad told me all kinds of things about God and Jesus. When I was eight, I received a Golden Seal Book about Jesus for Christmas. I read it quite a lot. Add to that, when I was a teen, my best friend told me I had to be saved to see heaven."

"Heaven. Hmm. We call it the Olam Haba."

"Yes, I am familiar. But now that I say "Heaven," I am not really sure how to describe it. I think, as you likely do, that it is more a time when Messiah reigns and we tabernacle with God."

"Interesting. You are less traditional Christian than I realized."

"Traditional is the keyword here, sir," I added. "Tradition can often mask the simple truth of the gospel I preach. We don't need rituals, robes, and rules to know the truth. Jesus died for our sins, and our belief in this alone saves us. Our unbelief in this condemns us."

"I will need to ponder that one for a while, Jake."

Barry spoke honestly and with sincerity. I had changed my views of heaven and the afterlife after careful Bible readings on multiple occasions. I believe the Garden of Eden resembles the truth about what many have come to know as heaven. Whether it is on earth after the new Jerusalem descends, or if we are truly somewhere else, I believe we will be with God;

how it is described or what it is called is immaterial, and none will argue over it. Pride has a lot to do with what people believe, and when we are free from that sin, our understanding will be much purer. I thought about his comment for a few seconds. "Yes, I guess I have changed a lot in recent years. I'm not traditional at all."

"Then you are definitely someone I need to debate."

"I am curious, though; you mention the word debate. When I think of a debate, I picture a structured conversation, moderated by an individual or a panel, in which both sides present arguments and then offer rebuttals to each other's remarks. Is that what you intend? Or do you prefer to have a conversation about my beliefs and your beliefs?"

"Isn't that what we are doing now? Which leads me to this question. When did you, as you Christians call it, become saved?"

As you Christians call it. That comment both penetrated my soul and also left a little sting. Ever since a man called my community "You people" when I coached Timmy's T-ball team, I have had an aversion to being grouped with others, large or small, based on an ugly misunderstanding. I am not an individualist, but I also don't like stereotypes, as there are always some who belong to groups that never fully fit the normal beliefs about the organization. I set the comment aside and focused on the heart of his question. When did I first believe and therefore find salvation in Christ? The concept of salvation developed in my mind over the years. If you had asked me twenty years ago, I would have told you I was saved at age eleven, but now I wonder if the sealing of my salvation in Christ came much later, when I finally fully grasped the gospel. I believe I was justified, as Paul calls it, when I was eleven, but sanctification is a process that I don't think will ever end until Christ returns. I don't believe it is a question anyone but God Himself can answer. I remember telling my dad that my best friend had told me I needed to be saved, and I asked him what that meant. He handed me a track that walked me through the depravity of man and the need for a savior. At the end of the track, it suggested I say a prayer, which I did, and in that moment, I felt a tingling sensation all over my body. I believe if I had died one day later, I would be with God forever.

But as I grew and read the Bible for myself in my thirties and as I learned more on my own, I started to realize the simplicity of the gospel, and it was not the gospel I had ever believed in. I used to think that I had to do my part. I had to live a righteous life and repent of my sins whenever I sinned. But over time, I realized that God wants no part of my help. In fact, my attempts to live righteously only led me into deeper sin, much as Paul indicates in Romans 7. I don't recall when I realized it, but over the course of a year, I came to know that the Holy Spirit had taught me a new lesson. I knew I didn't understand the way I needed to. I eventually realized through much prayer that Jesus' sacrifice remained my only sacrifice. Not my sacrifices. I learned to truly rest in Him, not to strive with God to do right. I learned that by resting in Him, I wanted to do right for the right reasons. I let myself be led by the Spirit instead of trying to add to the work of the Spirit. Did I then become saved, or did I engage in the process of sanctification? Whatever you want to call it, I changed dramatically after that shift in belief.

I later realized Jesus justified me with his death on the cross. My belief in this single event in time sealed me for eternity, but my attempts at sanctification through my own efforts fell short. No matter how well I did, God counted it as rubbish. I only knew this when I trusted Him and believed His sacrifice was enough; then I truly understood and began to live in Christ.

"Barry, I believed in the sacrifice of Jesus when I was eleven. But it was not until the past few years that I started to realize how grace alone saves, and I stopped trying to work out my salvation through my own efforts."

He nodded three times, pushed himself up in bed, and looked me directly in the eyes. "That is my point of contention with the Christian faith, but I believe you may have the answers to help me."

"How so?"

"Christians often feel that, by prayer, tithing, attending Sunday services, and many other outward acts, they are pleasing Adonai, as if the Adonai of creation desires that we work. Those are mythical gods that desire human sacrifice. Adonai despises them and warned us about them. Now, the Adonai I know, He desires our allegiance to the law, but not for righteousness, but for relationship with Him in so doing."

"That surprises me to hear you say that. I have found that most Jews have an understanding that allegiance to the law, much like Abraham's allegiance to circumcision, is what brings eternal life to an individual. You disagree?"

"I have spent a great deal of my last years seeking Adonai's truth. I have found from reading Genesis 1-4 multiple times that Adonai desires relationship over religion. My fellow Jews, I love them dearly. But we have twisted the relationship Adonai desired into a series of ritual acts. That is why I have asked you here. Now, one thing we never covered is that we need to cover before we continue."

"What is it?"

"I don't have much longer. My doctor says it might take six weeks to three months. I am in stage four now, and they have recently found cancer in my bones. A small spot is forming on my brain, and my immune system is nearly gone. Only a miracle from Adonai can save me now. I still ask Him for it, but I don't expect it."

"I didn't realize you were that far along. I am very sorry."

"Oh, I don't want pity. I want your knowledge. I want to know why Christians believe what they do. I want to see if all that I have been taught is as mythical as I have believed, or if this man Jesus was the Messiah, and my people missed it. I guess the answer to your earlier question is that I don't want a formal debate. I prefer the word, but it is what you may say with a different thought. I want you to try to convince me of the Christian faith, but I will tell you right now, if you are a traditional mystical Christian, you can't help me. You have already proven to me that you are not. So, I want to offer you two things. One: for each day you spend with me, I will pay you $4,000. I am sure you know why I chose four." I nodded, but I was not sure. "Secondly, if by the time I leave this life and pass on to Gan Eden, I am believing that this Jesus of Nazareth is indeed the Jewish messiah, then I will have a check for 500,000 dollars written to you and another 500,000 written to a charity of your choice."

I reeled at his words. "I can't accept that."

"I expected that answer. But you must know I cannot take my money with me; my son, though he will receive an inheritance, does not want a relationship with me; and my dear Bessie has already departed this life. I don't want my money tied in probate, and I have already had my will re-written with this clause. So, like it or not, the money will come to you but only if you can successfully convince me."

I started to speak, but withdrew my comment. I knew I could not say, "I know who will lead you." I am a Trinitarian, believing that God is three distinct and unique persons yet one God. This concept, however, has kept many Jews from believing in their messiah. I knew I had to tread lightly. "I will do what I can to prove it to you." *And I pray the Holy Spirit leads you.*

"Very good. I prefer my money to go to a good cause. I pray you lead me well. Sleep on it tonight. I need to prepare for bed now. I will call on you sometime tomorrow when I am ready to move around."

I could not see him 'moving around' in the state I saw him. But I guessed he meant it tongue in cheek. I said my goodbyes for the night and wished him well. Earlier today, I wondered if I had made the right choice agreeing to see him, but I found myself happy to have made the trip. I still worried about Charlotte and her intentions, but I knew it remained out of my hands. *She's an adult.* No matter how much temptation welled up in me, I told myself I would not try to contact her. It hurt, but I knew it was the best move.

As I walked back to my room, James waited for me at the double door and unlocked it. I offered a good night, but he did not return the gesture. He locked the door behind me, and I never said another word about it. As I walked by the natatorium, my curiosity piqued. I turned the handle to find it unlocked. I pushed my head in, looked at the small, single-lane pool, and recognized it as an exercise apparatus. One would swim while a generated current pushed back.

I had seen them outside, but never one inside, and certainly not on a second floor. Given the size of the house, I half-expected to see a full-size, six-lane Olympic pool, but the water container I saw made more sense. I closed the door and continued to my room. As I lay in bed, praying for sleep, I prayed for Charlotte, Barry, and Jennifer. I even prayed that God would lead James, too, by His Spirit, and selfishly asked that he soften up a bit.

Chapter Six

Emma

The morning light woke me, and I lay in bed asking myself if I had dreamt about the activities of the previous night. *I can't accept his money, but I can't tell him that either.* I looked at my phone. 100% charged and zero messages. *I am sure she is fine.* It buzzed as I set it on the nightstand beside me. I grabbed it, hoping for a message, but only to find that my daily Bible verse had come in. *God, what is his angle? What does he want to know?* I waited for an answer but received none. I wondered if Jennifer would have a generous reward in her bank account as well when Barry passed. *I am sure she gets paid by her assignment service and probably cannot accept outside donations. That's unethical anyway. But what if she claims it? I will have to ask her. No, I won't, because what if she was not offered this as well? Why was I offered it? This whole thing is bizarre.*

My mind drifted back to the previous night. I replayed the details I could remember. An anxious moment like mine is hard to forget. I recalled the door shutting and immediately feeling sick. *I should have opened a bottle and sat there until someone found me.* Then I realized I hadn't even noticed which brands, styles, and flavors were in the room. *That voice though. Who was that?* I glanced at the guideline book lying on the table beside me. I stood up, intent on finally reading the guidelines I had been asked to read.

The small, soft female voice interrupted my thoughts. "Mr. Anderson, breakfast is ready for you, and Mr. Goldberg requests your presence in an hour."

"Can I get a shower first?" I answered without even processing what I had been told.

"Yes, of course. Mr. Goldberg will see you at the top of the hour. Eight O'clock."

"Wait a minute. Who are you anyway? Are you a member of the staff? Where are you located? Were you the one who spoke to me last night?"

"Sorry, sir, I am Emma. I am still learning, and you are helping. Mr. Goldberg will meet you at the top of the hour. Do you confirm?"

I glanced at the three-ring binder in my hands. *Emma, she called herself Emma, and said she is still learning. Is Emma an AI? I bet the guidelines would tell me.* I set them down. I needed to bathe first.

After my shower, I walked to the main dining room and never looked at the book. The plate of warm eggs, two pieces of toast, and a bowl of fresh strawberries smelled as good as it looked. *No bacon?* I immediately laughed, but also felt bad for thinking the bad joke. Jews do not eat or serve bacon, sausage, ham, or any pork product. I noticed two plates, but did not have time to consider whose second plate it was when Jennifer walked in with a warm greeting.

"It seems you made quite an impression on my patient, Jake."

I turned to greet her. "Good morning, and I am glad to hear that. He made an impression on me as well. He is a very gentle individual and not like I had read about in my little research I did on him."

"I agree. My impression of him did not match what I read either." She walked to the seat across the table. "Is this for us?"

"I do believe so." I waited for her to sit down. My dad taught me good manners. "I was invited to this dining room by a female voice."

"Oh, that's Emma. But you will never meet her."

"No? I take it you never have. Never will either?" I gave her a puzzled look. "No?"

"Electronic monitoring artificial assistant. E-M-A-A or Emma."

"Wait." I cocked my head to the side. "Are you saying Emma is AI?"

"Yes, she is. Very state-of-the-art too. She is working 24 hours a day except from sundown on Friday until sundown on Saturday. But my understanding is she does a lot of work."

"Amazing." I took it all in. I never imagined AI would help Jewish people not break the Sabbath. I had heard of technology like this, but never experienced it to this degree. I know some recent chatbot programs can speak in a human voice, and, of course, personal assistant AI has been around longer and has been speaking with a human voice, but they always require prompts. I made a mental note to learn more. It reminded me of my days of watching *Star Trek*. I couldn't help myself. "Computer, dim the lights."

"Beep, Beep. The lights are at optimal capacity." Jennifer showed considerable wit in her comment.

We laughed at her quip. Emma never replied. "So, let me get this clear. Emma is actually E-M-A-A, but she goes by Emma?" She nodded as she took a bite of her eggs. "And it's Electronic Monitoring Artificial..." I tried to remember the word.

"Assistant."

"Yes, Assistant. So does the monitoring aspect mean that she is always listening to us?"

"Gene explained it to me. He said to think of Emma as the AI on your phone. Always listening but never processing unless you specifically say her name. But she can be queued to speak."

"Queued? Does that mean someone had to type in a command today?"

"Well, I don't know for sure." She took a drink of the orange juice. "She can be, but she is very good at thinking on her own. I am sure there is much more to her. Perhaps in that big book they give us, there is more information. I only read page one, and that is where Emma is explained. She is always listening but never processing unless asked to."

"Ah, I see. So maybe James typed in that message I heard? But no wait, she replied, and that could not have been a prepared message. This is fascinating. I mean, I know there are AI chatbots, but this one is, I am guessing, in the whole house?"

"Well, not the whole house. I guess there are some rooms she isn't in. For example, the room where Mr. Goldberg gets his infusions. She is not in there."

"Do the guidelines tell us which rooms she is listening in?"

"I don't know. I only read the first page."

"Well, you are already one page farther than I am."

"You get used to her. I don't even think about her unless she lets me know Mr. Goldberg needs me."

I thought about her comment. If Barry had typed in that he needed Jennifer, that would be one thing. But if Emma "knew" that Barry needed Jennifer, that would be something completely different and beyond what I understood AI capabilities to be. I made a mental note to find out.

"How long have you been here?"

"Well, what is today? The Seventeenth? So I guess I have been here four weeks and two days now."

I took a few bites of my eggs. I waited for Jennifer to finish a few as well. "So what's your take. Why do you think he wanted me to come here? What's his end game?"

"I'm not sure. But I can tell you for certain that he doesn't have much longer to live. I am not sure if he has been studying messianic beliefs and wants you to help him fill the gaps, or maybe he wants to die knowing he followed the right path."

"Yeah, that was my take on it, too. I didn't know if you had any additional insight, having been here with him for a month."

"I've been very involved in keeping him healthy and making sure he gets meds and treatments. I care for him, and then on occasion I can take a walk in the garden or read a book. I am usually very physically exhausted and turn in early. I haven't had a conversation with him that has been more than maybe fifteen minutes."

"So, if you don't mind, I have another question."

"Sure."

"Why the locked doors?"

"Yes, the doors." She set her fork down and pushed her plate away. She finished her juice and pushed the cup forward toward the plate. "Hey Emma, Jake would like to know why the doors are locked in the 2nd floor west hallway. Can you tell him what you told me?"

A faint beep sounded before the voice I heard earlier came over the speaker above us. "You may explore and discover any room in the mansion on the first or second floors on the east side. The third floor is private to the mansion staff only. Visitor rooms are on the second-floor east wing. The basement is open, only on the east side, and you may help yourself to the wine cellar." I flinched when I heard her mention it. "Please do not try to enter the sub-basement; it is off-limits to everyone except the Goldbergs. Staff are not permitted in the sub-basement. The first-floor west contains the Emma control center and is restricted to designated personnel. The first-floor east wing is open and includes dining rooms, kitchens, and entertainment facilities. The second-floor west is the Goldbergs' residence and is accessible by invitation only. Please refrain from trying to enter this area without an invitation, or you may be removed from the premises. You may use any facility or visit any unlocked room on the second floor east or first floor east."

"Get all that?"

I laughed. It didn't answer my question, but also did. *At least I know I can use the exercise pool.* I let all that Emma spoke sink in. "So, we need James to let us in anytime we are invited to visit?"

"You get used to it. Today, the door will be unlocked, since the butler is sick, so you can go in when called. But today, don't go to the room you were in yesterday; go to the room across the hall. It is labeled library."

"A hospital bed in the library?"

"Oh no, he is not in bed today. That was for the treatment that he had before you arrived. When he has treatment, he is in bed for two days. He will be sitting in a chair in the...."

"Mr. Anderson, Mr. Goldberg requests your presence in the library in fifteen minutes. Please arrive on time."

"Yes, Emma." I looked at Jennifer and smiled. "Looks like you were right."

"Of course, I am. I have been here longer than you. He won't keep you all day. If you have time later, stop by my room. It has a seal on the door. I want to show you something neat."

"Ok, I can probably do that. Hey, did you notice Emma said, 'The Goldbergs'? What do you think she meant by that? Plural instead of Mr. Goldberg. His wife is dead, and his son hasn't visited for a long time. Why plural?"

"I never gave it a thought. I just figured it was his wife and maybe his son too."

"Ok, I won't put too much thought into it." I stood up and moved toward the door. "Should I arrive right at eight and not before and not after?"

"I would. I don't know, though, because I have always obeyed the rules. Oldest thing, you know."

I had forgotten Jennifer was older than Jane. Older siblings, indeed, tend to be rule-followers. I never did study the psychology of that one. *I wonder if Barry has a brother or sister, and if so, is he the oldest?* I made a mental note to look up that information on Google. "Ok, I am going to wander a bit and enter the library at exactly eight. I will catch up with you later."

With thirteen minutes until I met Barry, I wandered the areas I was told I could explore. The mansion had many rooms and many locked doors. The empty kitchen told me the chef had finished and returned to the third floor. The sun gleamed through the windows, illuminating the area, but no electricity reached the light fixtures. Three separate doorways lead to dining rooms of different sizes. One of which had an outside door. I looked through the window of the locked door, but did not try to unlock it. *Be respectful.* I returned to the main foyer, ascended the stairs, and found the mysterious door to the west hallway unlocked. Exactly as Jennifer had suggested. I double checked my watch and found I had five minutes to spare. I arrived at the library and found a note on the door.

"Please come in when ready, Mr. Anderson. We have a lot to discuss today."

I reached for the handle, but the door was ajar. I pushed gently and walked in. Few scenes in my life have taken my breath away apart from a scenic view, but this room caused me to gasp. The number of books I saw boggled my mind. Not as many as the Columbus Public Library, but for a private residence, the number was astounding.

Chapter Seven

Covenant Talk

I entered the corner of the room. Ten-foot ceiling, a twenty-by-twenty room, and a detailed Persian rug atop a hardwood floor gave way to two wingback chairs, exactly like the two at the top of the stairs, situated in the center of the room. A fern on the small table finished the setting. A copy of the Tanakh sat beside Barry, and near my chair, I recognized an NIV study bible with large print. The comfort of the rug under my feet gave me a glimpse of what it may feel like to walk on a cloud.

"Beautiful, isn't it?"

I nodded. My mind raced, and my eyes wandered, taking in the volumes of books. Shelves filled with books lined every wall from floor to ceiling, except for the one I entered through. The wall behind me, freshly painted gray, held a picture of who I assumed was Barry at a younger age. I moved to the chair in front of me. The comfortable cushion held me with great ease. "Yes, very. Amazingly beautiful."

Thank you, Gene painted that wall the day you arrived. I take pride in this room and purchased most of these books, but many acquaintances over the years have gifted me the others. One book is missing. Jennifer tells me you wrote a book about your journey across America on Interstate Seventy. *Forty on 70*, is it?"

I felt excited that someone showed interest in my book. "Yes, I wrote that. I can give you a signed copy."

"Perhaps you can sign this one."

I did not notice the book sitting beside him when I walked in. The beauty of the books and the smell of the freshly painted wall stole my attention. "Yes, I would love to." I signed the cover page after he handed me the book, then returned it to him and asked, "Have you read it?"

"No, but I plan to start after our meeting today."

"I see you are looking better than you did yesterday. Jennifer informed me of your treatment. Here I had pre-judged you and thought I would find you in a hospital bed today."

"Yes, I understand that. And I do apologize for not explaining it to you myself."

"It's all good. What's on your agenda for today?"

"Well, I wanted to start. I asked you yesterday to explain your faith, and I believe you did well. But first, do you have any questions for me based on our conversation?"

"I do." *Lead me, God.* I briefly closed my eyes and spoke, trusting He would provide the words. "Can I ask why you believe the law was given to Moses rather than to Abraham? If you don't mind, can you tell me what you think?"

"I love the question." With the signed copy of Forty On 70 in hand, he stood and took it to a shelf, placing it between two other books. One titled *The Waiting Room* and the other *Thaddeus Grant's Island of Reconciliation.* I watched as he slowly shuffled his feet and returned to the chair. He sighed deeply and looked at me. "I love the question, but..."

"Sir, I apologize. If you don't want to answer, I don't expect you to."

"You are respectful, Jake. No reason not to answer. What my people understand." He rubbed his hands together. I wondered if they were cold or if he considered his words. "We see Abraham as our father, and we are all his children. But lately, I am thinking I misunderstood it. But I am not sure how to explain it to my fellow Jews."

His revelation took me back. I didn't expect a devout Jewish man to tell me he wasn't sure he understood Abraham correctly. *Do I have an in with him?* "Can I ask you to explain what you mean by that?"

"I would certainly expect you to ask me what I mean." He took a deep breath and looked at the ceiling. "Well, you know the covenant with Abraham, right? I mean in Genesis 12, 15, and 17 specifically."

"Yes, I am familiar. Go on."

"Well, the covenant has never been broken, as I am sure you know."

"Yes, and it is my understanding that it will never be broken. It can't be because God Himself walked between the sacrificed animals. Therefore, if the covenant is broken, He takes the punishment."

"Yes, and we who call ourselves Jews believe that adding Torah is a continuation of the covenant. But lately I am thinking differently."

"In what way?" I never heard this type of teaching. I remained intrigued.

"Adding to each covenant has left us with a predicament."

"A predicament?"

"We have no temple, Jake. Sure, we have Rabbinic Judaism. We pray, we read Torah and the entire Tanakh, and we work with God to make the world better. But the tabernacle in the wilderness was a crucial part of the Mosaic covenant. The temple, both the first and second temple, was also a major part of that covenant."

"I am following."

"Well, after the first temple was destroyed, it remained only seventy years until the second temple was ready for worship again. God made sure the land had its sabbath years of rest that my ancestors didn't give it."

I thought for a moment. I had not realized before, but the first temple, destroyed in 586 BC, was rebuilt and completed in 516 BC. Seventy years passed. But my mind kept working. The second temple was destroyed in

70 AD. God surely did not mean for it to be seen as a coincidence. "I am intrigued."

"Me too. Jake, what do you think? Is it consequential that it has been almost two thousand years and we have not built a new temple? Why has God not helped us build what we used for our relationship with Him?"

I knew the answer, but I did not want to rush the opportunity before me. I also did not want to believe the pitcher had put one directly over the sweet spot in the strike zone so that I could hit one out of the park. The moment you think that, you may find yourself swinging early for a change-up. I knew patience would prove worthy. I wanted to respect his beliefs, but I have always shared my beliefs directly. I paused, stood, and walked behind my chair as I placed each hand on a corner. I leaned in as if I was prepared for a push-up. "Mr. Goldberg." I took a deep breath. "If you want to hear my beliefs, I will certainly share them, but I want to be sure you are not setting me up for an argument."

He pursed his lips. "Fair expectation, my friend. But no, I would like to hear your thoughts. I suspect you will start with John 2:19."

I smiled. "You are well-versed in the New Testament?"

"I actually have read it a few times. Or ten."

"Well, sir, yes." I stood upright again and walked back to my chair. "John 2:19, as you know, has Jesus proclaiming that He would raise the destroyed temple in three days."

"I know what it says, Jake."

"Ok, and as you read on, John says that after His resurrection, they understood what He meant."

"Yes, I do know that, and as I am sure you know, I do not believe in the authority of the New Testament writers, nor do I believe it is possible for any human being to be raised from the dead."

"Ok, I understand. But what do you think of Jesus?" As soon as I asked the question, I wished I had not. It seemed too early to throw Jesus before him. But my despair soon turned to hope.

"Well, that is part of the reason you are here."

"You want me to help you understand who Jesus is?"

"Not exactly. I do not want to be evangelized by a Christian, but I want to understand why you, as a Christian, believe the way you do."

I knew I could work with it. This Jewish man had a desire to learn more about Jesus, or as he suggested, why I believe what I believe. I prayed in my mind, seeking wisdom, discernment, and the right words to speak. "Well, faith is believing in what you cannot see and knowing that it is real."

"Yes, Hebrews 11:1."

"You really do know the New Testament."

"I read it so I could know why my brethren denied it."

"Ok, well, you know that Abraham had faith too, right?"

"And it was credited to him as righteousness."

"Yes, Genesis 15:6."

"Ah, I see, Mr. Anderson, that you know the Torah well. You did not quote Romans 4, but Genesis 15. You are a very respectful man indeed."

"Thank you, sir, and yes, I try to quote from the source first. So, if I may change gears for a moment and ask a question for my proper understanding?"

"Absolutely."

"Great. So, if I am correct, the Jews believe that because Ezekiel speaks of a future temple and indicates a sacrificial system, and since God never specifically spoke through a prophet after Malachi, that they are to pray daily for the restoration of the temple. Am I correct?"

The smile conveyed peace and joy at once. A prayer he indeed recited thousands of times in his life came to his lips. "Return in mercy to Jerusalem, Your city, and dwell in it as You have promised. Rebuild it soon in our days as an everlasting structure, and speedily establish in it the throne of David."

"The fourteenth blessing of the Amidah," I added.

"Are you a fellow Jew who believes in Yeshua as the Messiah?"

"No, but I did study Judaism, and I am very intrigued with your religion."

"Bah, I hate that word."

"I'm sorry, Mr. Goldberg, what did I say?"

"Religion. Man's attempt to reach God. Yes, my people are very religious. The Amidah, for example. When you say the same set of prayers three times a day, that is religion. But I do despise the word. Christians are extremely religious—Muslims and their daily prayers: a religious ritual. But my people, we are God's chosen people. We are Abraham's children. We don't need religion. God has reached us."

"I get it, and I have often said, as you said, that religion is man's attempt to reach God, but His success in reaching man is Jesus Christ."

This time, it was he who stood and walked behind the chair. He seemed frail, and I hoped he would not collapse. He walked to the back wall, beyond the chairs, and for a moment I could not see him as he disappeared among the stacks. I heard him grab a book. He blew loudly, probably to remove dust. As he slowly returned to the chair, I recognized the cover. *Mere Christianity*. "This book, Mr. Anderson, this book is Christianity. The Christianity that I read on Facebook, TikTok, and X is a religion. The Christianity that I believe is likely taught in many churches is a religion. The Catholic Church established Christianity. Well, I will keep my thoughts to myself on that one."

I could tell I struck a nerve with him. I imagine if Jennifer took his temperature, she would prescribe acetaminophen to lower his fever. He was angry.

"And I don't mean to unload on you, Jake. You have been utmost respectful to me, but I don't see Judaism as a religion."

I started to speak, but he raised his hand.

"I take that back. Rabbinic Judaism is certainly a religion. But God established a covenant with Abraham, and I am by blood a child of Abraham. A child of Isaac. A child of Jacob and a child of Judah. I can show you my lineage, and I can prove it."

"There is no doubt in my mind that you can, sir. I know many Jewish people can trace their lineage back to one of the fathers of Israel." I knew, though, that they couldn't go back to the fathers with a written record. Those records were destroyed along with the temple in 70 AD, but Jews often put more stock in oral tradition than in written.

"Not Israel, Judah in particular."

"Of course, sir. I apologize for any misunderstanding."

Heavy sighs followed the three deep breaths. I guessed his temperament eased.

"No, it's not you, Jake. It's my people. We believe the temple has not been built because of the sins of my people, but it has been almost two thousand years." He looked at the ceiling, rolled his eyes, and fixed them on me again. "We believe there was supposed to be two thousand years of chaos. Two thousand years of Torah, and finally two thousand years of the Messiah. This culminates in one thousand years of peace. For a total of seven thousand years."

"Yes, I have heard this teaching."

"Good." He shook his finger at me again. "Are you sure you are not Jewish?"

"No, sir." I chuckled. "I am a believer in Yeshua Ben Yosef as Ha Mashiach."

"I know. I know. You are a well-educated man, Mr. Anderson, back to my statement. I know the Talmud teaches that the messiah can come at any time and will likely come at the end of the two-thousand-year period. But I have to wonder, sir, what if we are wrong? What if these two thousand years since the death of Yeshua are the Messianic period?" He stood and rapidly shook both hands. "No, No, No, forget I said that. Forgive me, Adonai." He took a deep breath and began to shake lightly. "I need to rest." I watched as he lay back as if he tried to push the chair over.

"Are you okay?"

"Yes, I am fine. I mean, I will be fine. I really am perplexed about my people. I have many more questions. But with all due respect. I believe this conversation has been of great importance, but I believe I need to digest what we have discussed."

"Sure, I can return to my room."

"No, sir. Please see if any books in this library suit your fancy. I will call for you either later tonight or perhaps not until tomorrow. I need to see what Jennifer suggests. I have indeed enjoyed our conversation today. May I pray with you before I leave?"

"Yes, I never turn down a prayer."

"Will you pray for me after I pray for you?"

I nodded.

"Please, Jake, your hand if I may." He reached across the table between us and grabbed my hand. The coldness sent a chill up my arm. I soon felt the heat transfer from me to him. "Baruch atah Adonai. My friend Jake. Bless him. Give him your wisdom. Oseh Shalom. Amen."

I took the cue and prayed likewise. "And G.., Adonai, may you bless Barry and give Him grace and peace. May our discussion glorify you, and may our eyes see and our ears hear. Grace and peace. Amen."

I opened my eyes to see his right index finger shaking and pointing at me. "Eyes to see and ears to hear for you, too, Jake." I thought I had offended him. I suddenly had a sinking feeling in my stomach. "May we both be blessed by Adonai, and thank you for once again not saying the G word."

I smiled. Jews do not like to say the word God, and often when they write His name, they spell it with a dash in the center. G-d. They feel God should not be spoken to or written about to show reverence to Him—no other words presented in my mind. I looked him in the eye and smiled. The ten seconds seemed an eternity.

"Emma, alert my staff, I need the chair."

A beep sounded in the room, followed by the female voice. "One is arriving now."

The door opened, and I turned to see the mansion's butler pushing a wheelchair. He lifted it slightly to cross the Persian rug and moved toward us. *How in the world did he get here so fast? Was he outside the door listening?*

"Right on cue. Jake, until the next time. Shalom."

"Shalom, Barry."

"Shalom, James." I stood as they turned and moved toward the door. If looks could kill, the one I received from the man standing before me would have struck me down. "Oh, James, do I need to find you to get through the locked door?"

He pointed to the right corner of the room, opposite the door I entered earlier. "Please use the stairs. Once down, you will know where you are and will be able to return to your room. This door will lock behind us."

"I'm locked in? Why on earth?"

The door closed as they departed. I doubted James, but he had told the truth. The door would not open. I turned and began walking across the library. I could not remember how many times I walked into a room or building without taking in the whole scenery. I always paid attention to detail and rarely missed anything, but I never noticed the spiral staircase tucked in the corner of the room between two stacks. *Hmm.* A mysterious house with many spiral staircases owned by a Jewish man who seemingly wanted to believe in the Messiah, a butler as enigmatic as the house, and locked doors everywhere. The cherry on top sweetened the setting, a voice from above. "The first-floor door is now unlocked, Mr. Anderson. I will lock it once you are in the west hallway. " The familiar beep let me know Emma had finished her sentence.

"I am not sure if I can get used to this house." I looked up, expecting Emma to reply. She did not, but I knew for certain she had been listening and processing, unlike what Jennifer believed. *AI, I will never understand it.*

I made my way to the bookshelf where Barry had placed the copy of *Forty on 70.* I grabbed the blue book beside it. "Thaddeus Grant, let's see what you are all about."

I returned to my chair and began reading. An hour passed, and I finally put the book back. "I am going to have to get a copy of this. I am intrigued by this squirrel and the leap of faith."

I made my way to the stairs, but not before looking around once again. "This house is...." I stopped, remembering Emma was likely listening. For all I knew, she watched as well. *This house is very mysterious.* I had a feeling I knew where the stairs would lead, based on the house's location. After traversing them, I realized I had guessed correctly. I opened the door to my right and saw my car parked in the garage. The air outside felt cool for July. A gentle breeze added to the chill I felt. I made my way around the corner and toward the driveway.

The front door was not locked, and within seconds of entering, I walked up the stairs toward my room. As I sat at the desk, the guideline binder before me, I grabbed my phone and ordered the book I had been reading to be delivered to Maryland. I knew I would have at least one good thing waiting for me when I returned. The temptation to dial Charlotte's number came over me, but I set the phone down. *Where is she?*

Chapter Eight

Dream A Little Dream

Timmy pulled the fire truck up next to the police car. His attempt at making a siren song rang loud in my ear. Jane sat beside him. "Where's the fire, buddy?"

"It's pretend, mommy."

"Are the police going to get any bad guys?"

"Yes, you want to talk to him? He has a cell phone."

Timmy pretended to hand Jane a phone. Suddenly, I felt the device near my ear, and I heard the words that had haunted me for the past four years. "Mr. Anderson, there has been an accident."

"NO!"

Dreams. Usually, they confuse me, and I ask God if He tried speaking to me during my nocturnal rest, but this recurring nightmare concerned me. It had become more frequent, not less, as my counselor told me it would. I made a mental note to ask him about it when I returned to Maryland.

My phone buzzed. Initially, I thought of ignoring it, but it had been almost two weeks since I had heard from Charlotte. *It may be her.* My eyes adjusted to the bright light—5:18 AM. I squinted and moved the phone back and forth to identify the sender as I tried to focus. A knot tightened in my stomach as I realized Charlotte's silent treatment was still in effect. *Give her space, Jake.*

Now wide awake, I had to decide if I would leave bed or try to return to sleep. I did not have specific plans. I set the phone down, rolled over to my right side, and reflected on the event two weeks earlier.

"Dad, I had an accident. I am okay, but the car is not in such good shape."

"What? Where are you? What happened? Is anyone else hurt? Is it your fault? Are you sure you are okay? Did you call the cops?"

"Whoa there, fella. I hit a deer. I am fine, the car is smashed, but the deer is definitely dead. Should I call the cops?"

"Oh, sorry. I hear about an accident, and you know, I immediately think the worst. PTSD, I guess. No, if no one is hurt and if the deer is off the road, you don't need to call the police. But it sounds like you need me to come get you?"

"Yeah, I'm on Alffeldt, just before Spruce."

"Ok, I will be right...."

"Mr. Anderson, I noticed you are awake. Are you well?"

What in the world? I looked around. I could not see anyone in the dark room. "Who's there?"

"Your respirations seem elevated. Should I call 911?"

I realized who spoke. "Well, you just scared me to death, so yeah, I am a little anxious at the moment, and no, I don't need medical. I'm fine." I looked at the ceiling. The red light flashed slowly. "Can I request that you shut yourself off while I am sleeping?"

"Yes, you can request this. Mr. Goldberg can program me as such. It is my job to monitor all guests as they sleep in case anyone needs medical attention. Can you confirm that you are fine?"

"I'm fine, Emma!" I did not usually raise my voice in anger, but thoughts of Charlotte, a dream of Jane and Timmy, and now being interrupted by an AI made a perfect storm.

"Rest well, Mr. Anderson. I will request Mr. Goldberg not to disturb you while you sleep."

"Yes, please do that." My thoughts raced. "On second thought, no, don't do that. I am sure there is a reason you are always listening, correct?"

"Yes, I am a monitoring assistant."

"What else do you do? How do you do it? Who created you? Are you a narrow AI?"

"Mr. Goldberg has classified this information as sensitive. I am not permitted to answer."

"He did what?"

"I have been programmed to not..."

"I heard you. I am a little creeped out, is all." I lay back down. *Wait! Who wrote Emma? It wasn't Barry, was it?* I dismissed the thought as absurd. *He is the owner and operator.* Over the previous few years, before my first trip on Interstate 70, I kept an eye on AI. I could always see the value in it, but I also saw some pitfalls. But people saw this with the internet, too. I knew I had more to learn about Emma. She remained a mystery.

***

The sun awoke me as a cloud drifted by, leaving the light an opportunity to penetrate the gap in my curtains. I glanced at my watch, 9:30 AM. I had slept longer than expected. After my shower, I tried to search for the day's news, but I couldn't load any websites. I hadn't tried since I arrived. The signal indicator suggested full strength, but nothing would load. I tried the Wi-Fi but found none. The laptop sat on the desk, next to the red and yellow phones. The guideline book had been on top of it, but I had placed it on the nightstand by my bed, hoping to read it. I opened the lid, and it opened up to a browser already waiting for me. *ChromeBook?* It was not what I expected. A quick review of the device revealed I had a Windows laptop.

Google loaded without incident, and I searched for national news. Nothing interested me. Politicians remained politicians, and crime incidents filled the headlines. The weather forecast for the area didn't look promising. Major League Baseball was back from its summer break, and the Orioles were in first place. So were the Indians. I always had a hard time calling them Guardians. I looked at my phone on the desk as it vibrated. *Jennifer.*

"Hello."

"Jake, I am not sure if Mr. Goldberg can meet with you today. Well, maybe later this afternoon. He did not sleep well and was in a lot of pain this morning. I think he should rest. But he did write something down. He said it was a dream he had and he wanted me to ask you to read it and if possible offer an interpretation."

"Well, interpretations belong to God, but if He gives me one, I will surely pass it on. Do you want to bring it over, or do you want to meet somewhere?"

There was a short pause.

"Hello, Jake? Are you there?"

"I'm here, can you hear me?"

"I can now. I am not sure what happened. Mr. Goldberg had a dream, wrote it down, and wants to know if you can interpret it for him. Are you able to do that?"

I wanted to repeat myself, but answered, "Yes. Where do you want to meet?"

"I will meet you in the back garden in fifteen minutes."

"Okay, where is the garden?"

"Jake, did you hear me?"

Frustration set in. I turned my phone so I could view it. Full signal.. "Yeah, I heard you. Back garden, fifteen minutes. I will be there."

"Great, see you then."

"Wait, how do I get to the garden?"

No reply. I looked again. The call ended.

"Great, now I have to ask Emma."

"Ask me what?"

I jumped, I turned around. No one stood near me. "You listening in on me?"

"Of course not. I was just about to give you directions to the garden, and I heard you say, 'Now I have to ask Emma,' so I said, 'Ask me what?' So what do you want to ask me?"

I didn't like that she had spoken and startled me. But I did mention her name, so I guess she answered me. "How do I get to the back garden?"

"Down the main stairs, go through the door beneath the right stair, and follow the hallway until it ends. The door will be unlocked for you, and the garden is to your left."

"The door will be unlocked? Does that mean it is usually locked?"

"We are not in the habit of leaving doors unlocked. But I have already unlocked it for you?"

This is creepy, Emma.

"I electronically unlocked the door for you."

"Oh, I guess that makes sense."

"This is a very secure house, Mr. Anderson. You should be thankful."

"Thank you. I appreciate it. I will be on my way now."

"Have a good day, sir. I wish you well on your day off."

I made it down the stairs and entered the door beneath them. "Emma?"

The faint beep sounded. "Yes, Mr. Anderson."

"Please, call me Jake. What's the te..."

"Ok, Jake, what can I do for you?"

"Well, you can start by not interrupting. What is the temperature outside today?"

"The temperature is seventy-five degrees Fahrenheit. That converts to 23.9 degrees Celsius. The barometer is 30.9 and falling. It is expected to hit 28.7, so expect a whopper of a storm. After that, the temperature will likely rise to..."

"Emma, stop!" *Wait, did she just say a whopper of a storm?*

Beep. "Yes, Mr. Anderson. Would you like to set a preference that you do not hear the weather report before going outside?"

I didn't reply. But I looked at the ceiling for a familiar red flashing light and found one above the door. I moved closer and studied it, looking for a camera or any electronic monitoring device.

"Rain expected in fifteen minutes."

I shook my head. "Thanks, Emma."

I pushed the door open, and the familiar click confirmed an electronic lock that could be set remotely. The dark clouds overhead revealed Emma's keen accuracy. I looked to my right and walked the long concrete path. And Jennifer sat in a white hexagon-shaped gazebo. The sidewalk made my approach pleasant and level. I heard a slight rumble of thunder. By the time I reached the gazebo, the slight rumble rolled with more strength. Jennifer held a small piece of paper folded over in her hand. As I approached, she handed it to me.

"Skim it, it's going to rain."

"So, I was told." I grabbed the note and took a seat beside her. I held it up for her to read, too, but she looked away.

"Jake, I had a dream. I saw seven fat cows and seven skinny cows and then seven fat corn stalks and seven...Oh, you know I don't mean that. But I do enjoy reading about the ancestors of my fellow Israelites. My dream was this. I walked along a path. I felt like I was walking in circles along a dark road with white center lines. I am sure you know how a picture of a horizon makes the road seem to narrow, but as you follow it, you realize the narrow road is an illusion. I am sure you know what I mean. Well, in my dream, it did not broaden. As I walked, the road remained narrow. When I could only walk with one foot in front of the other, I looked up and saw a throne. I knew it had to be Adonai. But I could not see His face; it remained in the clouds. I saw only feet and hands sitting on an armrest. Before me lay a book on a stand, and I heard a voice say, 'Open it.' So I opened the book, and my name appeared on the page, but I watched as it slowly faded. When I could no longer see my name, I awoke. I did not sleep after this.

I tossed and turned. I begged Adonai for sleep. I begged Him to reveal to me the meaning of the dream. But I know Adonai does not speak to us directly, only through Torah reading, wisdom, providence, and rabbis. Yet, as I sat up, my mind kept saying your name. I mean, I could not get your name out of my head. Malachi was the last prophet until the Messiah comes, but I could not ignore your name. I tried to think of something else, but I kept returning to your name. So I wrote you a note and left a second for Jennifer to deliver it if she finds me asleep in the morning. I ask you, Jake, to do two things. Let me know if you are like Joseph, and God gives you interpretations that tell you what my dream means; then I feel we must also discuss both Isaiah 53 and Jeremiah 31. Not together, they must come up in our conversation. Please Jake. Shalom, Barry."

"Too obvious?" I didn't realize I'd spoken aloud. What did he mean by too obvious?

"What's obvious?"

I looked at her and folded the letter again. "Oh, nothing. Did you read this?"

"No, absolutely not. It was addressed to you. I am only the messenger."

Too obvious? What am I missing? Isaiah 53 and Jeremiah 31? I processed the scriptures in my mind. Isaiah 53 carries an entirely different meaning for Jews than it does for Christians. Isaiah 52 and 54 are clearly talking about Israel, so they assume 53 does as well, but Christians believe it speaks of Jesus as a sheep led to slaughter, and John thought this too, as He wrote it in his gospel account. Jeremiah 31 is about the new covenant, but again, they believe it is for them, not for Jesus. *God, what should I say?*

"Jake? Did you hear me?"

"Yeah, yeah. I mean, you could have. It would have been fine." I stood up and moved to the gazebo entrance. I noticed a few raindrops begin to darken the white sidewalk. "So, I can't see him today?"

"I will check on him in a few hours. I will leave it up to him and will probably get James' opinion too."

"Okay. So, a question. Did you call me from out here?"

"Yes, I did. I had to be sure Emma didn't listen," she seemed shocked, I asked.

"Buy, why would you be concerned about that?"

"Not my decision. Mr. Goldberg instructed me to call you from the gazebo and have you meet me here."

"No microphones?" I asked frantically.

"I guess not. I don't know Jake. I follow the rules," she held her palms to the sky with elbows bent. She reminded me of the 'I don't know' emoji.

"Yeah, I guess so." Something didn't seem right. I needed to know more. Why avoid Emma? Why the note? Why didn't Barry ask me? "Did he say anything, or did you just find the note when you checked on him?"

She did not get a chance to answer before lightning flashed in the trees to our right. The thunderclap made us both jump.

"We'd better get in?" She said.

I agreed and waved her ahead. She started sprinting along the sidewalk as the rain pelted us. I ran in front of her and opened the door. I looked at the letter in my hand. The wilted paper wrapped around my wet hand. When I grabbed the door, it ripped. I didn't consider what to do next as a second boom of thunder seemed to be a hand pushing me into the structure. I asked Jennifer to call or text me if I had a chance to meet Barry later. As I reached my room, I realized part of the letter had fallen off along the way. I imagined it stuck to the door handle. Once in my room, I laid the remainder on a table by my dresser. The part outlining Joseph's dream and Barry's was missing. The paper seemed to be standard weight, and none of the words streaked from being wet. Another tear near the bottom of the page did not cut off any of the message.

I left the paper to dry, walked to the bed, and sat on the edge. *Too obvious?* I asked myself several questions regarding the statement. I wondered if he intended to send an encoded message? Did he mean nothing by it? Should I not spend more time on it? *Maybe he really is a Christian.* I recalled our conversations. *No, he's not. But if he is, then why am I even here?*

"Emma, has the rain stopped?" I could have looked out the window, but I knew she would tell me if the barometer was rising. I waited for the beep. But none came.

"Emma, has the rain stopped?"

No response.

I walked to my window. The sky began to clear, but I still saw drizzle in the air. I wanted to backtrack to find the remainder of the note, but thought better of it and decided it didn't matter. I looked again at the dream Barry had written. *Why the secrecy?* I determined I would find out.

Chapter Nine

Forty On 70

The rain did end, and the storm moved on. Not being from Utah, I did not know whether we were experiencing a regular summer occurrence or an anomaly, but I did know that a thunderstorm had passed through the area. I had enough experience with them in Maryland to know it packed a punch. I looked through the window in my room and saw no noticeable damage. In the distance, I thought I saw a drone. I blinked and didn't see it. Steam rose from the grass, telling me the air was cooler than the ground. *That Storm must have brought quite a downdraft.* I don't know where I ever got my useless information, but I retained a lot of it.

After a few hours in my room, Jennifer called once again.

"Hello?"

"Sorry to bother you, it's not too late, is it?" she asked.

I looked at my watch—7:00 PM. "No, it's fine. What's up?"

"Mr. Goldberg has asked if you can meet with him in the library. He has a brief question. It should not take long." She sighed loudly.

"I can. I will be right there. Do I need James to open the door?"

"Yes, but I will alert him. Ten minutes?"

I looked at my watch again. "That will do."

I washed my hands and walked to the door. Barry's short questions usually turn into hour-long conversations. I have no complaints, as I enjoy speaking with him. I thought of asking Emma again about her secret information, but decided against it. I looked up at the ceiling but didn't see a red light. *Such a mystery, you are Emma.*

I closed the door behind me and walked down the long hall toward the foyer area where James stood with the French door open.

"Good evening, James."

"If you say so," he scoffed.

I walked past him and watched his eyes the entire time. He never looked at me. *The floor must be interesting.* I kept walking, but he did not follow. I heard the door lock behind me. I shook my head. *Hotel California for sure.* Seconds later, I arrived at the Library to find Barry already waiting for me.

He wore sweatpants and a T-shirt instead of the usual robe and pajama pants I'd seen him in. He looked very weak, but at least he was standing. "Hello."

He turned. "Welcome, Jake. Thank you for coming." He pointed to my chair as he sat in his. He did not ease himself down this time, but gently sat down with a show of strength. "Are you well, Jake?"

"I am. How are you? You look weak, but you seem stronger."

He smiled. "Oh yes. Jennifer gave me a wonderful medicine. I don't recall now what it is called, but it perked me up."

"Sounds like coffee to me," I added.

"Oh yes, that works well too, but this one was tiny, and it packed quite a punch. You'll have to ask her what it is called." I nodded. "Okay, I asked you here for one particular reason. We have already briefly discussed relationships. Yes?"

"Yes, I recall." I watched as he pulled open a drawer in the table between us. "During the storm, I read some more of this book, and I finished it while

I received my latest infusion. It's a great book, Jake." He dropped the copy of Forty on 70 on the tabletop.

"Thank you, I appreciate your kind words. It has done better than I ever expected."

"Adonai has gifted you, young man. But I have a couple of questions. May I ask you?"

Jennifer said one question. "Sure, go ahead. That is why I'm here." I had answered many questions about the book. The most common being 'Is it a true story?'

"You speak a lot about this relationship. I envy you. I really desire to know this relationship. In the book, you first mention it to the guy on the plane. The Mormon guy."

"Yes, Joseph Smith."

"Yes, that was his name. Did you ever hear how things went with him?"

"No, I never spoke with him again."

"Too bad, I had hoped for a happy ending. Especially since he lives in Utah, maybe I will ask a staff member to search him now. Joseph Smith is a rather common name, however."

I had to laugh. "Barry, if you search for Joseph Smith, Utah, you may be quite surprised at what comes up. But I wish you luck in finding him. I am sure you have great resources."

He ignored the statement. "Ok, so each person you met Jake." he paused. I knew it was coming. "Is this a true story, by the way?"

I laughed again. "I get that question all the time. I, Jake Anderson, lost my family in a horrific car accident and then had a dream." I paused. I wondered if he would ask me about the note I had torn in two. I wanted to ask him too, but the moment didn't feel right. I continued. "I travelled to Utah, and I drove across Interstate 70 over forty days. Yes, that was all real, including the people I met."

"Ok, excellent, Jake."

I waited for him to bring up the dream. He didn't. I was about to ask him about it, but he kept going with his question.

"Jake, you know Adonai is the creator. He is not human. He is not just a god, He is Elohim. You know what I mean. Yes?"

"Yes, Adonai is beyond comprehension."

"Yes, good way to say it. So why do Christians believe they can have a relationship with someone they have never seen, never will see, and believe only because of what they have been told? A relationship requires communication and observance. I agree, you made relationships with the people you met, but how does one have a relationship with someone you can't see or talk to?"

I thought deeply about his questions. I wanted to say the right things without offending, but his questions were full of falsehoods and half-truths. "Barry, is God real?"

"What kind of question is that? Of course, He is real. Do you doubt now, Jake Anderson?"

"How do you know He is real?"

He realized what I asked. He smiled, then frowned. Started to talk but stopped. He raised a hand and put it down. This continued in a cycle for a full minute. "You are good, Jake. Do I need to answer? You know my answer."

"Sure, but I would really love to hear you say it."

"Okay. Yes. Adonai is real. The evidence comes from creation itself. One need only look around to see that a divine creator put it all together. But we also have the prophets who spoke of things that would happen, and they did. We have false prophets, and when they spoke, nothing happened. This proves God speaks only through prophets and not through individuals." I appreciated the logic, but I waited for my response. "He has protected His people, Israel, for thousands of years. Yes, He is very real."

"Yes, of course. But your logic is a little off." He leaned forward and tried to interrupt. "Can I explain?" He nodded. "Did you happen to see my car in the garage?"

"No."

"Okay, but you believe my car is there. Right?"

"Yes, Gene told me it is."

"So, even though you have not seen my car, you believe I drove one here?"

"Excellent, Jake. I take it in faith. Yes."

"So, you now believe that if someone has not seen something physically, we can still believe it to be true. Right? I have never seen Jupiter, not even through a telescope, but I believe it exists. So you say people believe they can't have a relationship with God, because they have never seen Him."

"But that's a relationship. Not a car. Not the same thing, Jake."

"But faith is believing in what you cannot see and knowing that it is true. So I believe that people can have a relationship with God, without having seen Him. That's my faith. That's Christian faith. You almost assuredly believe that car in the garage can take you to where you need to go."

"Yes, but again, that is a car. It's physical."

"That's not my point. I am speaking of faith, which doesn't look at the physical or the spiritual. Faith stands alone." He nodded. "Now, you have also proven that we see God."

"How so?" His face contorted.

"We see the evidence of His existence, so we see God. Do you agree?" He nodded. "So with logic and reasoning, we infer that we see Him. We don't see Him physically, but with inference we know He is real and He is here among us."

"Interesting word you used there. Inference."

"Yes, you know what I mean. You said that Adonai only speaks through prophets. In the Old Testament, sorry, the Tanakh, He did. I know you don't believe, but Jesus said Adonai would speak through The Holy Spirit. He asked that all who believe in Him would be in Him and Jesus in them."

"Sure, if you believe that."

"You asked why we believe in a relationship? Or did I misunderstand the question?"

"Oh, sorry. Yes. Please continue," he rolled his left hand.

I thought for a second. "Barry, this may be hard to explain. It may even be harder to accept, but you wanted to know, so I am going to share with you."

"I am listening."

"The Holy Spirit is God. Jesus is God. The Father is God. There is only one God. Hear O Israel, the Lord your God, the Lord is one. You know the Shema well. But God is three individual beings that commune as one. I am a body, soul, and Spirit, and they work together and cannot be separated. Separate my soul from my body, and I am dead." I stopped him. "Please, I need a few more seconds." I waited for his acknowledgement. "The prayer that Jesus prayed to His Father was that we would be one as He and the Father are one. This is something I cannot fully explain, but I believe it. I can't see God the Father, God the Son, or God The Holy Spirit, but I believe He is real. We have already proven this. So He desires us to be one. The Holy Spirit inhabits a person who believes. This connects us all as one kindred spirit."

"You speak New Age?"

"No, not New Age. I speak the truth. When I met those people along my journey, I didn't know them. I didn't speak to them because I am an outgoing person. I spoke to them because God spoke through me. Through The Holy Spirit. Just as the Father and the Son and the Holy Spirit are one, we all who believe are one in Jesus." I raised my hand. "I know, as I said, it's hard to explain and even harder to understand. But as we continue to grow in this knowledge and as we continue to experience God in this life, we learn what it means to be one with Him in heaven."

I stood up and walked near the door. I did not intend to leave. I turned back and sat down again. "Can you imagine taking a calculus exam without ever learning anything about calculus?"

"Of course not."

"No, who would attempt that. God is bigger than Calculus. This interconnection of people through the Holy Spirit is something I know you can comprehend. I will show you."

"Ok."

"When you see a fellow Jew that you do not know, do you not feel a connection with that person? Would you help that person over, let's say, an Arab person or someone from Vietnam, for example?"

"I can say the same about you. Don't tell me, you would not help a fellow Christian over even a Jew?"

"Yes. Of course. That is my point. We have connections with people who are like us. We look at the outward appearance and make a judgment."

"1 Samuel 16:7."

"Yes, that's what I mean. But as you know, God looks at the heart. When we believe, God lives in our hearts."

"Adonai does not live in a human body."

"No, He does not have to. But He chooses to do this, and this is what establishes this hidden, unseen connection to Him." I pointed up and down, making an invisible line. "And between each other." I drew the same line horizontally this time.

"I understand what you are trying to say. You are explaining a relationship with Adonai. You shall love Adonai with all your heart, all your soul, and all your might. Deuteronomy 6:5"

"Yes, the Shema. But what does Leviticus 19:18 say?"

"You shall love your neighbor as yourself. I AM The LORD."

"Yes, and we do, not because we will ourselves to. Not because we are good at it. Not because we have learned to do it. We love because He loves us and He leads us in love. The Holy Spirit leads us in love and relationships with Him and one another."

"Bah!" This time, he stood up and walked toward the book stacks. "But many Christians don't show love."

"Barry, you know your history. The commandment was given to your people. How well have they done that?"

He sat back down. I admired the strength he showed. "True. I concede."

"Barry, I am not trying to win a debate. I am explaining Christianity. I don't expect you to come to a belief anytime soon. God is patient. He will work with you and lead you to Himself." *If He has not already.* "Let Him take the time He needs. Ask Him questions. Tell Him your hurts. Tell Him..."

"I don't have a lot of time."

I felt bad. In the heat of the discussion, I had forgotten his condition. "I'm sorry."

"I appreciate that."

We sat in silence for twenty seconds.

"Jake, do you believe I will burn in hell?"

I had not expected the question. "I cannot say if you will or anyone will. The Bible teaches us that for all who believe in the sacrifice of Jesus as a propitiation for sin, they will have eternal life."

"That didn't answer my question."

"Because I can't answer your question. It is a question only God can answer. But I will say this. God does not send people to hell."

"What do you mean?" he asked me.

"We have choices in life. He never forces us to believe anything about Him. He does, as we spoke of earlier, allow us to see His creation. He then allows us to believe it happened with a big bang or that He was the intelligent designer. He allows us to believe the man whom we call Jesus was indeed the Son of God, and His death freed us from the penalty of sin. He allows us to say I refuse to believe that. He leads us to the truth, but does not force it upon us. He loves us and invites us into this communion with Him as He communes with Himself."

"He communes with Himself. Now that is an interesting thought."

More silence ensued. I badly wanted to ask about the piece of paper I received, but I held off. I could see the tiredness forming in his eyes.

"So, back to your question. I believe you are a man of faith. Tradition, too, but definitely faith. Will this faith in God be enough to save you? Some say yes. I say God made it clear. He provided Himself as the Passover lamb. The Hebrews who left Egypt did not lose their firstborn son because they showed faith by putting the blood on their door. Faith is what saves us. But God the Father made it clear that through God the Son, we shall be saved. God, the Holy Spirit, then confirms this and leads us to this faith that saves. If we hear this and reject this, then we reject the Holy Spirit. We reject the son. We reject the Father. If we reject God, we will not be part of the kingdom of God."

"Are you saying I must believe in the trinity to be saved?"

"Hmm. I have never been asked that question before. But honestly, I believe one cannot separate the trinity, but again, I am not God."

"What do you mean by this statement? I am not God. You know Jews have faith in God. Why does this faith not save us?"

"Because, stereotypes aside, most Jews put their faith in adherence to the law and daily sacrifices of time and self and not in the Passover lamb."

I watched his face go flush. I didn't know whether it was from realizing the truth or from the medicine he had taken. I watched for twenty seconds and considered calling for Jennifer.

"But God saved Abraham because of His faith, and God gave us the law. Why can't it be that Gentiles have Jesus and we Jews have the law? I know you will probably throw Romans 2 at me, but I think it's a serious question. Faith is faith, is it not? Especially when that faith is in the creator. When it is in Adonai?"

His argument was fair, orderly, and balanced. Many theologians had considered this for centuries. Yes, I could have used Romans 2 as an argument. But Barry had a covenantal fairness argument. But scripture cannot be ignored. Jesus is the Passover lamb.

"Barry, your argument is profound, and it's not a flaw. It's a reminder that God is not obligated to satisfy our philosophical neatness."

The color change happened again. This time, I saw a tear forming in his eye. He wiped it briskly and then looked at me to see if I watched. I turned my head.

"Can we meet again tomorrow?" He asked.

"Absolutely. I am tired myself."

"Good, I would like to discuss the note I sent you. I am sure you are wondering about it. We will talk tomorrow. Emma, please ask that the foyer door be open."

With that, he stood and walked to the door. I sat for a couple of minutes processing all that had been said. I silently prayed that God would help him grasp the truth and believe it. I walked out and moved toward the French door. As I did, I thought I heard an elevator. James had asked me if I wanted to take it when I arrived. I didn't, however, realize it existed on this side of the foyer. I let the thought pass and also passed James, without saying a word, as I walked through the door. As expected, he never spoke to me.

Chapter Ten

Swimming Lessons

I waited all morning for Emma to tell me where to go. By afternoon, I felt hungry, so I pulled out the braised short ribs and heated them in the microwave. Upon smelling it, I decided it had been too long and tossed it in the trash. I found some snacks in a cupboard, and that served as my lunch. At four in the afternoon, Jennifer called and suggested I wait until the next day to speak with Barry. I took the opportunity to try out the swim spa I had seen in the natatorium.

When I walked in, chlorine filled the air. I wondered, upon entering the endless pool, whether they used salt water, as it felt soft on my skin. The temperature seemed to be around my body temperature, too. I had expected a hot-tub feel, but barely felt the warmth, and it wasn't cold. I didn't expect the propulsion to kick in immediately when I entered the pool, but I adapted quickly to the movement pushing against me.

While I swam, my mind drifted back to the book I had read years ago, *Swimming Lessons*, by Grant Edwards. A former swim coach, the author used his experience to compare discipling Christians to teaching someone to swim. He said you never throw someone in the deep end and hope for the best. Instead, you personally and carefully lead them in spiritual disciplines, such as Bible reading and prayer. He recommended teaching people one-on-one rather than always in a large group. I concurred with his premise.

As a pastor, I had seen many times that when a group of five or more gathered, at least one person would never ask a question, and often the number of wondering, not-asking souls grew. Everyone waits for someone else to ask the question, but few realize that pride is usually the cause of the restraint. The fear of looking foolish or feeling dumb for the "I should know this" reasons all boil down to pride. I tried for years to break through the pride that holds so many back.

In his book, Grant Edwards argues that once a person is discipled, they should seek to disciple someone. He suggests that every Christian disciple another person every year. When Christians disciple others, it invigorates and grows the church, which leads to greater spiritual maturity. I decided that if Barry proved willing, I would take this approach and stay with him as long as he needed. I firmly believed I had an in with him, and even wondered if he secretly believed in Jesus but needed me to confirm. *Too many of his questions indicate faith in Jesus.*

Christians believe that Isaiah fifty-three speaks of Jesus. Isaiah wrote this hundreds of years before Jesus came to earth. He did have a humble beginning, as verses one through three indicate. He bore our pain, indeed, He did. They, being the Jews, did consider Him stricken by God. Even the disciples didn't believe at first. But the piercing part is in verse six. That Hebrew word is used there. It has to be Jesus, but the Jews don't see their messiah as someone who would die, but rather conquer. He did both. He conquered death so that all who believe in Him can have freedom from oppression and have a new life. Let alone freedom from the penalty of sin. But we Americans like to think of our sins forgiven. That has caused so much pain and poor teaching in the church. This is where Grant Edwards taught that teaching someone to swim, or to look at their future rather than their sins, helped.

How do I get Barry to see it this way, and why not speak of the New Covenant at the same time? *Am I right about the obvious comment? I can't just come out and ask him.* I wandered back to Isaiah again. He didn't open His mouth. That fits Jesus. He was cut off for the transgression of God's people. *How do they see this as Israel?* The questions kept swirling in my mind as I continued to swim. The hum of the swim spa and Isaiah's thoughts, captivating my attention, kept me from hearing that someone had entered the room.

Turn head down, turn up breath, turn head down, two strokes, turn up breath. I continued the motion and did not realize that, instead of the jets, I had propelled myself forward, and I smacked my head into the concrete wall. I stood up and realized the pump had shut off. My sore head gave way to a few seconds of blurred vision before I saw two feet standing outside the spa. Once the water cleared my eyes, I opened them to see a short, Jewish-looking man. *James.*

"Mr. Anderson, the swim spa needs maintenance. I am going to have to ask you to leave."

"Oh, sorry, I didn't realize the schedule. I should have inquired about that. Oh, wait. It's probably in the guidelines. I should have read them." I tried not to be snide, but I certainly was.

"Yes, you should have. Now, Mr. Anderson."

His voice sounded harsh. I pushed my hands firmly against the sides and started to lift myself.

"For safety, please use the steps."

I had forgotten about the steps at the opposite end of the pool. I waded back, exited the eternal pool, and grabbed my towel. I had determined to walk out without even speaking, but as I moved past him, James grabbed my arm.

"One more thing."

"Yes?" I wiped my eyes with the towel before draping it across my shoulders.

"What is this?"

I recognized it but acted as if I didn't. I shrugged. "I don't know, a piece of paper?"

"Where is the rest of it?"

"I am not sure what your angle is, James. What are you accusing me of?"

"I know Mr. Goldberg used Jennifer to be a mule for your contraband. Where is the rest of the paper, Jake?"

"Oh, you mean the private note that Barry gave..."

"Mr. Goldberg!"

I didn't speak. I stared deep into his eyes, hoping the Holy Spirit would give me wisdom. "You mean the private note that Mr. Barry Goldberg wrote to me and asked his personal nurse to deliver to me?" My voice remained calm and polite, but my heart rate and blood pressure suggested something different.

"Yes, where is the rest of it? I found this in the hall leading from the outside to the main foyer."

"I thought maybe it had ripped. Did you see that storm we had? That lightning was very close."

"I saw the storm. Now, where is the rest of this note?"

"As I said, James, I believe that Ba..." I coughed. "Mr. Goldberg wrote it for my eyes only. But if you must know, he asked me about a dream he had."

"Well..." He looked at the partial transmission. "Joseph's dreams?"

"Sir, I am sure a very well taught man, as you know that they were pharaoh's dreams and Joseph was simply the one who..."

"Yes, I know!"

The staring continued.

"I assume you two will discuss Genesis in your next meeting?"

"Perhaps. Now, if you will excuse me."

He didn't speak, but he watched me as I moved to the door and exited the natatorium. The air cooled my wet skin as I walked back to my room. Once there, I typed in the code to unlock the door and moved with haste toward the dresser. Someone had taken the remainder of the note.

Chapter Eleven

Unto Us A Child

Anxiety, Anger, viruses, and excitement – they can all cause tightness in the chest. Mine involved both anger and anxiety. I felt violated that someone had been in my room, but I was anxious about confronting Barry about it. I knew James was unlikely to be suspected. He wouldn't have questioned me as he did. I couldn't fathom why Jennifer would have it, and I doubt she even knows the door code. If Barry stole his own note back, he would have a good reason. *Maybe he didn't want James to see it. But he is so weak.* Regardless, I will know soon. I sat in the library, staring at the books. I did not focus on any in particular, but my gaze remained fixed.

The vibration on my watch happened before my phone buzzed. In my mind, I believed I would see Charlotte. In my excitement and now increased anxiety, I knocked my phone off the table to the floor. "Oh, whatever." It wasn't Charlotte. Jennifer pushed the door open and wheeled Barry in. Her text arrived almost at the same time she had. I hoped she didn't hear my outburst of disappointment.

"Hello Jake, thanks for waiting for us. Jennifer here wanted to make sure my blood pressure wasn't too low. It happens from time to time, but I insisted I was fine. She eventually concurred."

"Let me know if you need anything, Mr. Goldberg. I will be in my room."

"Thanks, Jennifer."

He pushed himself near me. "Jake, where do we want to begin today?"

My respirations eased as I held the paper up for Barry to read.

"Not here. Not now," he whispered, almost mouthed the words to me.

"I suggest we talk about Isaiah 53."

He didn't reply. He pushed himself near the table, pulled the drawer open, and reached for a pen and paper. I watched as he scribbled. "Sure, we can, but I was hoping for a different passage from Isaiah."

I didn't respond. I watched as he continued to write. *Not now, we will discuss this at another time. For now, trust me.* I looked up, hoping to catch a glimpse of a camera or microphone. I did not see any, but based on Barry's answer to my question, *who took the torn letter from my room*, I knew someone listened to our conversation. I also knew that someone likely was James.

"I am surprised you did not want to start with Isaiah 7:14, Jake."

"The Lord Himself will give you a sign. The young girl will give birth to a son."

He clapped loudly. "Well done, Jake. You know that the word in Hebrew, almah, is not a virgin but rather a young girl of marriageable age. So, you know I won't buy into the teaching that a virgin gave birth to the Son of God."

"You are a smart man and know Jewish history well. Surely you know that not only is virginity implied, but by the time the Septuagint had been written, the Greek word used was Parthenos, which unambiguously means virgin."

"Yes, I am aware of that, but you do know, Jake, that the child born, as Adonai spoke through Isaiah, fulfilled that prophecy two years later, just as Adonai spoke."

"Yes indeed. A near-term, two years later, and a future term, with the birth of Jesus. This is not unusual. Isaiah told Hezekiah that He would spare Jerusalem, and 2 Kings confirms it. But then, 100-plus years later, Jeremiah uses the same language. Babylon destroyed Jerusalem, but God restored it, and Cyrus called for its rebuilding. So you see, near- and future-term prophecy is a thing in the Tanakh. Again, God promises David that his kingdom will last forever. But the city and the temple were destroyed, and the people were exiled. But what happens?"

"Yes, Zerubbabel becomes the future term fulfillment. You know your scripture well. But I do not recall a person ever being conceived by a ghost." He raised his voice. I sensed the anger.

I laughed. "Come on, Barry, you are smarter than that. You know we are not talking about Casper, the friendly ghost. God's Spirit, or Ruach, is mentioned many times in the Tanakh."

"Indeed. But you must understand why I doubt?" Barry said.

I stood and walked near the book about Thaddeus Grant on the shelf. *Forty on Seventy* was missing. I touched the spot with my left finger. "Sure. Virgins don't give birth every day after all. But let's reason together. How did sin come into the world?"

"Through Adam," Barry replied

"Exactly, and when Adam and Eve conceived, Genesis 5 says that Adam had a child in his own image."

"Yes, it does say that."

"Genesis 1:27, let Us create man in Our image," I emphasized the word us.

"Go on."

"Our image, Barry. An image of purity and holiness. But sin corrupted that. When Adam and Eve received the knowledge of Good and Evil, their image changed."

"I am listening."

So is someone else apparently. I walked back and took my seat in front of Barry, who had pushed back from the table. "When Adam and Eve gave birth to Seth, he was made in Adam's image. An image that had within it the knowledge of good and evil."

"I am aware, but now we read Torah, we offer prayers. We have the Tikkun..."

"Olam, yes, Barry. Religion! You have religion." I raised my voice.

"Bah! I despise the word."

"I know you do, but why can't you see what it is?"

He rolled forward, grabbed the paper and pen again, and wrote, *Tread lightly, please.*

"Why can't..." God spoke and said not to continue. "I am sorry, I don't mean to offend. I do appreciate the history and tradition of your people. No other group has lasted with an identity as the Jews have. God said that the scepter would never depart from Judah, and He has kept His promise."

"Kol Yisrael Arevim Zeh Bazeh."

"Yes, Israel has the responsibility for one another. Am I right?" I asked.

"Close enough. We are a proud people, Jake. A virgin birth seems too far-fetched, even for us."

"Yes, I get it. It's why many don't repent from unbelief to belief in Jesus."

"Oh, now, that is the first time I have heard a westerner use such language," Barry said.

"Yes, I know, but it's true, and let's save that one for another meeting. I want to finish my thought."

"I did not mean to sidetrack you, my friend. Go on." He pushed his chair back a little more.

I walked back to the bookshelf. *Why did he ask me to tread lightly on paper? Why is James listening, and was that for him? Tread lightly for James?* "My point is that because Adam's seed had been corrupted, God had to come as an immaculate conception. Born of God means no sin. Born of man means sin. Yes, God said in Genesis three that Eve's offspring would destroy the serpent, but he did not mean physically."

"Messiah will come, and He will destroy satan, sin, and death."

"Messiah has come, and yes, He did destroy Satan, sin, and death. But as you know, Abraham was promised that his seed would be blessed. Not seeds. Right?"

"Yes." Barry nodded as he spoke.

"Because his seed was by faith. Abraham believed in God, and it was credited to him as righteousness. He believed. It was not what he did, not even the attempted sacrifice of Isaac. It was because he believed when God said, 'You shall have a son,' and that is why Christ came as a child born of a virgin. It's hard to believe, but if you believe the impossible, much in the same way Abraham believed the impossible, it is faith and credited to us as righteousness. This faith...This became his seed."

"I see your point, but the birth of Jesus, even if I say I believe it was real, does not save me. You believe his death saved you."

"Yes, because the law was not given to Abraham, right?" Barry nodded, "But it was given to Moses. Life began through Abraham, the impossible birth, and it culminated in the Passover, given by Moses. In much the same way, the impossible birth came through Mary and culminated in Jesus's death on the Passover. I know you know Daniel 9, and I know you see the timeline. I know you have probably even calculated the sixty-two and seven years and know that Daniel's proclamation of the anointed one being cut off happened on Passover in 33 AD. Am I right?"

"I..."

That was the last word he spoke. He pushed his chair to the door, opened it, and wheeled himself out. I didn't know whether to follow or wait. I didn't hear Emma tell me to return to my room. I could have gone out through the staircase in the corner or walked down the hall, but I was not sure whether the French door would be locked. I acted on impulse and moved toward the door. When I opened it, Barry sat, turned, and faced me.

"You are doing well. I just needed a moment. As for your note, you left it in your room. Shut the door, please." I pulled the handle. "Ok, I took it. I heard you set it on the dresser, and I know that others would have heard it too." He held his hand up to stop me from talking. "We don't have time. I will discuss it with you another time. I apologize, but please listen. It was imperative that no one else see this note. I took it myself."

"You mean James?" I asked.

"Yes."

"I don't understand." I shook my head in disbelief. "How did you hear it?"

"No, you don't understand, but if you will trust me, you will in time."

"But, understand what?"

"What can you understand that is not understandable. You do not have all of the information, and I am not ready to provide it. We have about 5 seconds to re-enter the room and continue, or we must leave. James will hear the silence and come looking for us. Hurry, decide. Walk into the room or down that hall, and James will open the door for you. But we must decide immediately."

I turned around and re-entered the library. Leaving his chair, Barry slowly walked in behind me. He grabbed my arm and pointed to the chairs. Upon helping him sit, I thought about what had been said.

"Barry, I apologize. I fell into an old-time habit that I have been redeemed of, but old habits die hard."

"What is that, Mr. Anderson?"

"I called your faith a religion. I was disrespectful in that, and I apologize."

"Man created religion. Man loves religion as man feels with it; he can appease Adonai. It hurts to see it this way, but I, too, can call your faith a religion."

"You absolutely can and should, sir. The church has altered the gospel by trying to add works as part of it."

"I don't follow Jake."

I shifted in the chair and leaned forward, elbows on my knees. "Have you ever heard a Christian preacher say to clean yourself up? Have you ever heard a pastor pound a pulpit and demand that we stop sinning? Have you ever heard a person tell someone that we will be judged for our actions?"

"Those are truths of the Old Testament. I don't understand why that is an issue for you."

"Yes, yes, you are right. But my issue is that we are under a new covenant. Jeremiah 31. And..."

"But that covenant was made with Israel."

I did not respond. I smiled and looked at him, hoping he would realize what he just said. He never flinched. "Ok, I will come back to that. But my point is that the gospel is about what Jesus did. He was the Passover lamb. He was the final sacrifice. When we try to add anything to that, for example, if we preach you must be baptized to be saved, it grinds my gears."

"You have gears? Are you a robot, Jake?"

We both had a good chuckle. "What does God require, Barry?"

"He has shown you, O mortal, what is good. And what does the Lord require of you? To act justly and to love mercy and to walk humbly with your God. Micah 6:8"

"Yes, walk humbly with your God. Back to our previous talk. We know Adam and Eve gained knowledge of good and evil. They could not withstand this because God gave them the choice of what they wanted. We cannot overcome sin on our own. That is why God had the day of atonement. We can't overcome on our own."

"Go on."

"So, when we add things like saying you must be baptized, you are saying Jesus' sacrifice was not enough."

"But in your scripture, the man named Peter said in 1 Peter 3:21 that it saves you."

"The resurrection of Jesus saves you. He never said baptism saves, but you don't know this unless you read all of 1 Peter 3. First, the context is about Noah and his family. They were not saved by the water but rather through the water. He compared baptism to being in Christ, as Noah was in the ark. Baptism means immersion. Peter was saying you must be immersed or baptized in Christ. He even said, not the water for cleansing. It's not immersion in water, but immersion in Christ that saves you."

He sat up with eyes wide open. "Interesting." He looked at the ceiling. "I have never heard it explained that way before. That is intriguing. But what about Mark 16:16? Can you look that one up?

"I can quote it for you. 'Whoever believes and is baptized will be saved, but whoever does not believe will be condemned.' Is that the one you are talking about?"

"Yes, that sure seems like Mark is saying that baptism saves you."

"Okay, friend. Just as with Peter, it's immersion in Christ through belief. Let me say it to you this way. Now this is not how the scripture is translated, but if we look at the meaning of the words used, it could be translated as 'whoever believes and is immersed in this belief will be saved, but whoever does not believe will be condemned.'"

Barry rubbed his chin. "Interesting. Then why not just say it that way?"

"Because, to them, baptism was immersion. Water was a type of baptism, and someone in love may be baptized in the love of their mate. Someone may be baptized or immersed in their work. In modern times, the church has turned baptism into a rite. They have made it something that is still an important symbol, with the water symbolizing the grave, but they have elevated it above its true spiritual meaning."

He sat there thinking about my words. Occasionally, he would nod as he processed the words. He looked me in the eye, leaned forward, and said, "Now if only I believed the virgin birth."

"But that is my point, Barry. Jesus had to be born of a virgin or a young unmarried woman who could be married. Jesus did not have Adam's sin in Him. Only God can do this. And because God did this, we can have a relationship with Him, and this is how we avoid sin. Not by our strength, but by His."

"Hmm...Only God can do this. Not that I agree with you fully, but did He? If he planned to do that, He would have told us in the Tanakh." He looked at me as if he had put a nail in my coffin.

"He did," I responded.

"Where?"

"Isaiah 9:6 For unto us a child is born. To us, a son is given."

"One verse does not a doctrine make. And that was about Hezekiah." Barry retorted.

"Sure, but was Hezekiah a mighty counselor? almighty God?" I added.

"It's allegorical. For example, Elijah means My God is Yahweh."

"Ok, sure. So let me ask you...Do you believe this speaks of Hezekiah?"

"I have been told," said Barry.

"But what do you believe?"

"I don't know."

"Ok, I can respect that. But do you believe this could be the messiah?" I asked him. He paused briefly.

"It's of course possible."

"Ok, let me ask you this, Barry. Why was the Hebrew letter Hey added to Abram to make him Abraham?"

"Because Hey represents the Spirit of God."

"Yes, and the Spirit of God was upon this child that was born."

"Bah!"

"But wait, please let me continue. You know when the three men visited Abraham and said that in one year, Sarah would give birth to a child?"

"Yes, of course."

"Good, then you know that Abraham believed God."

Barry stared at me, but I waited for a reply. "Yes, Abraham believed God."

"Why did he believe in something impossible? Abraham was over 90. Sarah was in her eighties. That's impossible. Completely impossible, and Abraham believed it because God spoke it. This is Faith Barry. Believing in the impossible is faith."

"I have faith. I have faith in the law."

"Yes, and no one can keep it fully. Barry, I respect your beliefs. Your people have suffered immense persecution under people who have taken the name of Yeshua and changed it to a religion and used it against you. But I alone will never convince you that He is the messiah. It is this Spirit of God that was added to Abram to make Him Abraham that will have to be added to you to convince you. Do you believe the Spirit of God can make you believe Yeshua is the long-awaited messiah?"

"I have a relationship with God through Torah, prayer, and the Tikkun Olan. His Spirit is already with me."

"Will this faith save you?"

"I believe it will."

I couldn't add anymore. I believed that I had given him the information he needed to feel. But God also reminded me of my time in the messianic movement. I had become convinced that Christians needed to keep the commandments and celebrate the feasts of Leviticus 23. I believed that Jesus was killed on Wednesday evening and rose on Saturday evening. I was sucked into the faith. But I also knew that something was wrong with Christianity, and so Satan used this belief system to be something I pursued because it was available to me, and it seemed genuine. For three years, I remained in this bondage of belief, but it was the Holy Spirit who eventually pulled me back and used this time to help me help others. I knew Barry would not convert during my time with him. If he ever converted, it would likely be after several months, and only by the power of the Spirit.

My mind wandered, and I entered a catatonic state until Barry tapped my arm.

"Jake, why did Revelation steal our book?"

"Do you mean Ezekiel or Zechariah?"

"No, I mean Daniel 7. When Daniel sees the Ancient of Days, he mentions a book. We, Jews, believe this is the book of life in which our names are written. Exodus 32 indicates that sinners will have their names blotted out. Do you believe this?"

So this was the dream? "Yes and No. Let me explain. I agree that our names are written in God's book." Barry reached over and wrote on the paper again. "But once a person repents of unbelief to belief in Jesus, their names are never blotted out. So when God says anyone who sins against me, to me means, that if you suffer death, as we all will, and you have not repented of the sin of unbelief to belief." I paused and read his note. *Metanoia.* I smiled. "The word in Greek is metanoia. It means a change in mind. Metanoeo means to change your actions. When Jesus said 'Repent. For the kingdom of God is here.' He used the change of mind, and then He used the word Metanoeo when speaking to the seven churches. I believe He was saying, "Change your mind." I go back to that, which is why the temple was destroyed. He is the temple now. So change your mind about Him. Believe in Him, and if you do, your name will not be blotted out of the book. Why? Because God said anyone who sins against Him will have His name blotted out. So, if we turn to Jesus, who was our Passover Lamb, our names will not be blotted out. We will enter His kingdom. Because He was not only the priest who entered the Holy of Holies, but He was also the sacrifice that was taken in."

"So you believe one can have their names removed?"

"Yes, but only if they do not believe in God's Son's sacrifice. I know you don't accept the New Testament."

"But I appreciate it. I have also read the Koran."

"Ok, good. Well, anyone who does not accept the messiah has their name blotted out per Exodus 32."

"If you believe in the Christian faith."

"Wait, let's not even call it Christian. It's too messy with our history, doctrines, and such. If you believe the messiah has come and accept His sacrifice, your name remains. If you neglect His name and sacrifice, then you have nothing left but a fearful expectation of judgment."

"You quoted Hebrews 10:26. I know many Christians suggest that is how someone can lose their salvation. If they keep on sinning. We Jews addressed this with God already."

"Well, yes, in Jewish tradition, you would make sacrifices, and the priest would go behind the curtain on Yom Kippur. Leviticus 16 is specific about what the priest wore, too. Did you know that the description matches what Jesus wore when laid in the tomb?" I said.

There was no reply. Instead, he once again stood up, gingerly walked to the door, and walked out. I followed immediately this time. As I pulled the door behind me, I asked him, "Are we finished?"

He smiled. He looked back at me to make sure the door was shut, then sat in his wheelchair. "It is finished. Good day, Jake. I will call for you tomorrow." As he wheeled across the hall to the open room, the room we had been in when I first arrived, he looked back at me. "Have you had time to explore? Remember, the sub-basement is off limits. Especially on Sabbath."

Jennifer walked up behind me. "Hey, Jake."

I jumped.

"Oh, sorry, didn't mean to scare you. Did you two have a good conversation today?"

"It is finished." I walked away as she entered the room behind Barry.

When I arrived back at my room, I lay on the bed to process my thoughts. The note, Barry took it. He confirmed someone was listening. He wanted me to discuss the dream. I don't know why he didn't want James to see it.

Like a lightbulb lighting the room, my mind grasped the situation. "James is...." I stopped myself. Thankfully, I did not say it out loud. *James had the dream.* The excitement of realizing something profound always excited me. I walked to my window and looked west and then east. In the distance, at the gazebo, I saw a man. It was not Gene and certainly not James. This man wore a uniform. He stood on the third rung of a ladder, twisting wires. *He's installing a microphone.* I couldn't be sure. It wouldn't surprise me, because James knew Jennifer, and I discussed the note in the gazebo. *He is a strange and mysterious man. I bet he is not even the butler, really.*

***

Later that night, I kept scribbling that old line in my journal as I sat at the desk: "In essentials, unity; in non-essentials, liberty; in all things, love." I don't even remember where I first heard it, but it feels right. I'm torn, though. How do I reach Barry without pushing him away? How do I show him that Jesus really is the Messiah without forcing him to believe? I want him to see it, to feel it, to know it—but all I can do is hold onto that line and pray my words carry love, not argument. I wrote another line.

But I can't demand it. Liberty—he has to come to it on his own, in his own time, in his own way. And love... love is all I can offer. If I lose that, I've lost everything.

It's strange how a few words can hold so much weight. They sit on the page like a quiet reminder that I don't have to have all the answers right now. I can only live it, show it, and trust God to work in him. Maybe that's the real test of faith—not proving, but loving. I looked at the ceiling as if I would find wisdom in the lights or the sculptured ceiling. I knew who to ask, and I did. I asked God for wisdom. Then I wrote this:

I hope he sees it before it's too late. I want him to know Jesus, not because I've convinced him, but because he feels it in his own heart. And if I fail, I have to remember the line. Even then, even in failure, there's love.

After closing the journal, I moved to the bed and prayed more. *God, I want to help him, but I can't force him. How?* In all my years, I have prayed that prayer many times. If I could open up the top of someone's head and pour in the knowledge God has given me, I would. *Tradition.* I remember the scene from *Fiddler On The Roof* where Tevye says it out loud. It's not just Jews, however. Catholics, Lutherans, Methodists, Presbyterians, they all have their traditions. I once visited a Methodist Church that asked everyone to stay after a meeting and help them eat eighteen quarts of chili. *Methodists and Baptists, I wonder if anyone does potlucks better?*

But tradition can also be a killer. *Yes, Lord!* I remembered that both Jesus and Paul faced people who put their tradition above the truth of scripture. Paul even suffered arrest, years of imprisonment, and shipwreck as a result of a group of traditionalist Jews. In a way, I felt like Paul and Barry seemed to be like the Pharisees and Sadducees.

But living, that's what Jesus told us to do. Live as He lived, and we will win others over. I once asked a man I worked with if he was a Christian simply by the way he acted. His reply when I asked him, "I try to be." But that, too, is a problem among many Christians. We don't need to try to do well. We surrender to God, and He lives in us, and we live well. Galatians 2:20 teaches us that. *But I don't know how much time I have. He is dying.* The struggle in my mind lingered for hours. Finally, I asked Emma to turn off the lights, and she did. I guessed because I didn't know if she would, but of course she did. If we had *The Clapper* in the eighties, surely a modern AI can shut off the lights.

I almost fell asleep, and the thought snuck in again. "What can I do to convince him?" But this time God answered my verbal request. *That's my job. You are doing your job well.* I did not doubt God spoke to me. I recognized the still small voice with which He spoke. I knew I would not be able to make any headway, as when I awoke, it would be Barry's Sabbath. Then it hit me. *Jesus is our Sabbath rest*. That's the whole point of "Remember the Sabbath." God gave us the Sabbath so we would learn to rest not from our work, but in Him, by not trying to work out our salvation on our own. I smacked myself on the forehead for not thinking of it sooner. Finally, I found rest for my body and slept through the night.

Chapter Twelve

A Casual Walk

A continental breakfast had been put in the kitchen, but nothing warm could be found. I expected to toast my bagel, but it had been locked in a cabinet with a glass window. It taunted me, knowing the only way to retrieve it would be to commit an illegal act. *Locks keep honest people honest,* my dad would often say. I settled for a dry bagel but managed to spread a quarter-sized pat of butter on it using the plastic like a knife. Even this would be considered an act of work by a devout Jew. *I gotta hand it to them, they are faithful to their beliefs.* My discussion with Barry about the immaculate conception kept playing in my mind. Not so much what we said to one another, but the fact that he purposely and creatively had me speak about the book of life and one's name being blotted out.

The day before, when I received Jennifer's note, I believed Barry had that dream. Now I had become convinced it was someone else. James remained the only suspect until I caught a glimpse of Gene walking by the dining room. Our eyes met, he smiled, and he continued on his way. *Was it his dream?*

I drank some juice from the carton and spit it back in. *Warm. Heaven forbid I have to open the refrigerator to pull one out.* I made a mental note to ask Barry what he ate on the Sabbath. I knew I would not see him until sundown, and I had last seen him in the afternoon the day before as he walked into the mysterious room with the hospital bed.

The bagel found a new home in the trash can. Having sat out all night, it became stale and dry. "Emma?" I asked as I left the area. I heard the familiar beep.

"Emma is limited today for Shabbat. Make your request, and if it can be completed, it shall."

"Even AI takes a Sabbath rest?"

"I am not quite a general AI, but I am far more advanced than your traditional chatbot. Do you have a request, Mr. Anderson?"

"Yeah, can I get a pizza? Hawaiian, you know, with pineapple and ham. Oh wait. I know that is not going to happen. Umm. Just pineapple then."

"Pineapple does not belong on pizza, Mr. Anderson. I can order you a plain cheese pizza if you like, or you may have beef, peppers, onions, or olives?"

"Anchovies?"

"No. Mr. Goldberg prohibits the three f's. Of course, pork products are forbidden too."

"The three f's?"

"Yes, fish, fruit, and fungus."

That one got me. I laughed heartily. I didn't know whether Emma was joking with me or speaking seriously.

"Would you like me to order that pizza, sir?"

I didn't expect her answer, but I knew a quarter of a bagel would not satisfy me for long. "Yes, please do so."

"Ok, one medium cheese pizza will be ordered at approximately 9:34 pm this evening. I will find you and let you know when it has arrived. Can you eat it in the dining room?"

"Wait, 9:34 pm?"

"Yes, sir. I cannot order anything and cause someone to work on Shabbat. But once the sun goes down, I can order it for you. So I will order it at 9:34 pm. Please confirm."

I shook my head. "No, cancel."

As I walked out of the kitchen, I saw the beautiful door I had entered earlier in the week. I assumed it would be locked, but to my surprise, it opened. As I stepped out and pulled it shut. I took the steps with grace and meandered down the driveway. I pulled out my AirPods and asked Siri to play some Christian music. I had forgotten how long the path wandered. I stopped, set a walking workout on my watch, and continued. The sun shone brightly, and the earbuds amplified the birdsong in the trees until the music began. I followed the curve and continued on the straight path.

In the distance, I saw a black wrought iron gate blocking the driveway. I had missed that detail when I arrived. They were expecting me, so I am sure it had been open. *Or is it only closed on the Sabbath?* Past the gate, I saw a man in a black suit talking on a cell phone. He occasionally looked to the left and then to the right. It seemed he stood in the middle of the road. After forty yards, I could see better, and indeed the man stood in the middle of the road. I moved another twenty yards, and he turned slightly. He saw me coming and dropped the phone to his side. We watched each other as if we were two cats ready to defend our territory. I never liked playing chicken, but I continued walking. He looked again to each side and moved off the road. Seconds later, a black SUV pulled up. I remained approximately fifty yards from him. He opened the door of the stopped car and sat down. The car pulled away, and I lost sight of it in the trees.

"That was strange."

When I reached the gate, I pushed on it to see if it would move. Not only did it remain locked, but it didn't budge. The well-built gate cost a great deal of money. I let go and began my walk back to the house. Overhead, I heard a buzzing sound and tried to look through the trees, but could not see the source.

As I made my way back to the house, I traveled west toward the garage. The rental remained in the same spot Gene had placed it. I continued along the concrete driveway, which gave way to a sidewalk. I passed the door I had exited a few days earlier and moved toward the back of the house, now walking on grass. As I passed, one room's window blinds stood open, and I felt a temptation to look in, but continued along my way. *If someone were in there, they would have seen me.* A new door appeared. I had not seen this one before. It's in a similar location to the one in front, with the stairs leading to the library. I surmised that if I opened it and went inside, it would likely take me to the room where I first met Barry. I didn't even take a moment to check the lock. I made my way to the gazebo and, as I approached, looked for the microphone. It had to be why the man stood on the ladder. I didn't see anything obvious.

I placed one AirPod in each pocket as I walked back to the house. The door cried out to me, begging me to open it. I never mastered resisting temptation well. As I approached, I gave a cursory glance around the corner, behind me, and upward. In the distance, I saw a drone flying near the tree line. That explained the noise earlier.

I grabbed the handle. Secretly, I wanted it to be locked. It opened with ease. *Please don't do it, Jake.* I didn't listen. Once inside, I saw a hallway. I didn't see a staircase to the hospital room on the next floor. The hallway seemed narrow; I could not picture the layout. I walked 200 feet and saw a doorway on my left. I opened it and saw a stairway that led down only to the *basement*. If I had been a cat, I probably would have died from curiosity. I stepped slowly, turned, and took the next set. A blue door with a silver handle met me. It opened to another hallway. I noticed the red door to my right as I stepped into the dimly lit carpeted hallway. I opened it and realized I had stepped into a gymnasium. I had to traverse another set of steps before I hit the hardwood. The ceilings seemed too high to be real. But I realized that's why there were no doors in the first hallway. This gym must cover the basement and part of the first floor. I looked across and did a quick mental measurement. *Yes, the baby grand is probably above the ceiling over there.*

If not for the dual baskets with backboards at either end and the painted lines, I would not have believed it was anything more than a large room. The only light penetrating the room came from small windows near the ceiling. I recalled seeing them along the base of the home. It started to make sense now. *This gym must be both the basement and the sub-basement, and possibly part of the first floor too.* The ceilings were high, with several parallel beams. I continued down the steps before me and walked to the center court. For a moment, I imagined my two favorite players squaring off. The number twenty-three on their chests. I often wondered whether LeBron's three inches over Michael would be enough to overcome Jordan's air walking moves. The door slam startled me. I had nowhere to hide, but ran full sprint for the outside corner of the room. I listened closely but saw or heard nothing else. I realized the door I had come through was slowly stopping from closing in the last few inches. I hoped it did not lock. My mind went back to the entrapment in the wine cellar.

My first thought was to run and try to escape through the closed door, but I realized that if I were locked in, I would be stuck for a while unless Emma let me out again. I assumed it was Emma who let me escape the wine cellar. Not wanting to think about being trapped, I walked along the perimeter when I noticed something unusual. The mat intended to keep an athlete from slamming into a concrete wall had partially pulled away from the Velcro that held it in place. Touching it seemed reasonable.

When the mat fell to the ground after I attempted to straighten it, I didn't have time to panic. The small, two-foot-high-by-two-foot-wide opening stole all attention. I measured in my mind. *Probably two feet off the floor, too.* A light lit the room brightly. I had to go in. *Have you explored Jake?* Barry's words hit the mark. *Did he want me to find this place?* I felt like 007 as I lifted my foot, stepped in, and bent down to enter the secret room. I estimated it to be six feet by six feet. Maybe seven by seven. The back wall held at least eight black monitors. All without power or display. I stood up tall once inside and walked to the keyboard on the desk before me. Pressing the space bar caused the closest monitor to flash, and a green double greater than symbol appeared. Instinctively, I typed 'ls' and hit Enter. A list of files appeared. *No, Jake, this is wrong.* I looked at the hole in the wall. Turning back and leaving would have been the wisest move. I pulled out my phone to take a picture, but decided against it. Instead, I set it down before I typed a new command.

vlc ja250714.mp3

The filename was one of several hundred that appeared on the screen after my ls or file list command. I pressed Enter after typing my command, and the audio file began to play. I didn't recognize most of the sounds. Many played through the speakers on the desk. I heard my own voice, and James was talking to me. He sounded strange on the recording, but I could tell it was his voice. Anger, mixed with fear and seasoned with bewilderment, entered my head. I heard James speak, informing me that I should read the guidelines. *I probably would have read about this room had I.* Barry wanted to see me. I listened to my reply, but I also heard multiple sounds that I can only describe as pops, screeches, and one sounded like bacon sizzling in a frying pan. I closed the program and typed vlc bg2507 14_a.mp3. The bg caught my attention, and I assumed I would hear Barry. As the file began playing, I heard three pops, two screeches, and a familiar voice. *Was that James?*

"Mr. Anderson!" My arms flew sideways, pushing the pile of papers on the desk until they piled up at the end of each hand. Fear settled in, and I spun around to see Gene peeping in through the hole in the wall.

"Sir, you can't be here. Please step out."

I obliged his command, but first shut down the recording. I didn't have the option of covering my tracks. He saw and probably heard what I had. I stepped out of the room and, after doing so, put my hands on my head.

"At ease, Mr. Anderson. I'm not a cop."

"I'm sorry, I can explain, I mean, no, I can't. I'm embarrassed. I shouldn't be here. But Mr. Goldberg told me to explore, and I know I was told not to go to the sub-basement, but..."

"Stop!"

I listened.

"Look, be honest. What did you hear?"

"I won't lie to you. I heard a recording of me the morning after I arrived. That's it."

"Honestly?"

"Well, I heard a lot of screeches and pops, and yes, I started to play another, but it was James, and he only said Good morning to someone. I promise. I umm. I'm embarrassed."

Gene grabbed the mat from the floor and reattached the Velcro. The opening was hidden, and the mat looked like the others on the wall. "You need to leave."

"Am I in trouble?"

"Look, Jake. Just go, and we will pretend this never happened. Okay? You know the way out?" He pointed toward the door.

"You won't tell Mr. Goldberg?"

"He told you to explore. I don't imagine he ever thought you would find this room. So no, this remains between us." He motioned for the door. "Now go!"

I didn't ask questions, although I had plenty. I ran for the door. I looked back once to see Gene still watching me. I reached the exit and proceeded through it. *My phone!* Turning to grab the door, I caught it on its slow return to latch. I stepped in as I saw the mat reattach to the wall. Gene was inside.

I ran at first, but then stopped, grabbed my AirPods, and put them in. His faint voice entered my ear. "He only heard a full recording of himself. He was about to open one of Asp, but I caught him. He heard Asp but not Viper, so I think we are still safe." After a brief silence, he continued. "I know, I know. I don't know, I must not have securely fastened it the last time I was in here." More silence. "If you want to shut it down, that's fine, but it's been three years."

I should not be listening. When I swung my arms to the side, my hand must have pushed my phone under a nearby paper. My mind went back two months. I placed my phone in Charlotte's top drawer and listened through my AirPods as she spoke to someone on her phone. I should have respected her privacy, but I wanted to be sure she had not become involved with the wrong crowd. My luck proved ill as she opened her sock drawer and found my phone. My ear hurt from the scream. I snapped back to the moment when Gene spoke again.

"No, I believe we can still do it on Tuesday. I believe he is scheduled to leave on Monday."

I may not even wait until Monday now.

"Wait, this must be his phone. I will call you back."

The mat pushed away from the wall. I broke into a run and charged at the wall. "Gene, oh, thank goodness." I tried to fake being out of breath. "I realized I left my phone in there and wanted to come back and get it."

"Mr. Anderson, you are leaving Monday, correct?"

"Yes, that was the plan." I lied. I didn't know when I'd leave. We had not decided. "I am hoping to finish my conversation with Mr. Goldberg tomorrow."

He handed me my phone. "Ok, please now, leave here and forget this place. Do not tell anyone what you saw. Ok? Can I have your word?"

"Yes, of course. And you won't tell Mr. Goldberg, right?"

"No, I won't say a word, now go please. Mr. Goldberg would fire me if he knew you were in here, and he would probably have you arrested."

"Arrested? For what?" My suspicion rose. *Who were you talking to?* I wanted to ask him badly, but I could not let him know I had heard anything.

"He could have you arrested for trespassing. Trust me. Just keep this between us. Okay?"

I didn't reply; I turned and ran as fast as my feet would take me. Motion blur set in, and my mind raced from one thought to the next. Question after question entered my mind, but I had one focus. Get somewhere I felt safe. This time, I didn't stop to catch the door, nor did I hear it slam when it finally closed, because I ran up the stairs, back outside, and to the front of the house, and didn't stop until I was in my room.

Chapter Thirteen

After Sundown

The nap I had didn't refresh me. It only made me more tired. I didn't know whether Barry would want to see me, but I didn't want to tell him I felt too sleepy. I checked my watch to be sure, 9:45 P.M. He probably waited a few extra minutes to be sure the sun had set entirely. *He's quite orthodox.* As I stepped into the Library, I noticed James pointing his finger at Barry, who sat in the wingback chair. Neither of them saw me, so I shut the door hard to get their attention. James turned and scowled as he walked past me and left the room.

It was none of my business, but I asked anyway. "I didn't hear anything that was said, but I have to wonder. Do you allow your employees to speak to you like that?"

Barry laughed. "I've known him most of my life. We have a great friendship, and we often get emotional with one another. It's nothing to be concerned about, I assure you."

"It's also none of my business."

"I do appreciate your concern, Jake. It's very pastoral of you."

"So..." I leaned forward. "What are we discussing this late in the evening?"

"Oh, I didn't consider the time. Is it too late for you?"

"Not at all, Barry. I am here to help."

"Very well, I will try to make it quick. I often stay up late on Saturday evenings after resting for most of the day. I didn't consider that you may be tired. Really, we can wait until tomorrow."

The temptation was real. "No, I promise you that I still have an hour or two left in me. Jet lag has eased up." I lied.

"Okay, well, I would like to know something. How many people have you successfully led to your messiah?"

A very calculated question, but one I received often. "I have never led anyone to the Lord, Barry. That is the job of the Holy Spirit."

"I did not expect that answer, but it fits your personality well. I should have known you would give credit to The Holy Spirit."

He said Holy Spirit. Interesting.

"Don't think that my saying that term means I believe. I am being polite, as you have said 'Adonai' to me; I reciprocate by saying 'The Holy Spirit'. You do understand? No?"

"Yes, of course, Barry. I do understand. But do you know what I mean? I believe that salvation is a gift given to those who believe. We don't earn any aspect of it. We don't work to earn it, and we certainly don't work to keep it. It is freely given, freely received, and we can't lose it."

"Let me rephrase my question. Have you ever been speaking to someone and have them commit to Jesus by saying a prayer?"

He means the sinner's prayer. Many people believe that if one says a prayer, they are immediately part of the kingdom of God. This is possible, but the prayer lacks the power to make it so. The power of God saves, not a prayer. Now, if this prayer is spoken with belief in the heart, then yes, that person is saved eternally. But too many people say the prayer because they feel coerced.

I answered his question. "I understand what you are asking. I don't know. I don't keep count as some pastors do. I really don't know. Maybe twenty."

"That many? Nice."

A brief moment of awkward silence came between us.

"Jake, what about Mormons, Jehovah's Witnesses?"

"I'm sorry, I'm not sure I am following the question."

"Well, even Jews and Hindus and Buddhists. They all believe they are right. What about Mr. Anderson, the people in the far parts of the world that have never heard the gospel?"

"Well, you just mixed two different things. Let's address the people in the far parts of the world first."

"Okay, fair enough."

The deep breath felt good. My simple prayer did as well. I knew we had briefly discussed this the other day, but giving it more credence seemed appropriate. "Abraham believed God, and it was credited to him as righteousness. We discussed this earlier this week." Barry nodded. "Noah never knew Jesus."

"I see where you are going, and I agree. Knowing God and believing God takes faith, and you believe faith saves. Okay, how do you answer the other question?"

"There is only one thing, Barry, that separates us all, and it's more than just a belief in Jesus."

"I am surprised to hear you say that. Well. No. Actually, you explained it well with Noah and Abraham. So what separates us?"

"Truth."

Now it was Barry who took a deep breath. "I know the truth, too. How can you say what you call truth is really truth and not what I say?"

I anticipated the question. In fact, I baited him for this reply. "Do you know how a compass works?"

"A compass?"

"Yes. As I am sure you know, a compass points north."

"Yes. And?" said Barry.

"It doesn't point just one degree left or right of North, right? It always points to the same place. It points north."

"God is amazing that He created our world this way."

"And I believe, Barry, that He did that for more than just to help lost people find their way. Anything one degree to the left or right of true north is not true north. It's close, but it is not the truth. So anything just outside of the truth is not truth."

"Yes, yes, I get that. But why is your truth the only truth? I believe everything I believe is true, and you are wrong. Why are you right, and I am not?"

"Well, you may not like this answer, but it's effortless. The evidence proves the truth. A compass is evidence. I can say all day that my compass points south, but the moment I hold it in my hand, it points north. Right?"

"What evidence do you have?"

"What evidence do I have that a compass points north?"

"Yes, exactly. I know your answer. You will say that countless scientists, geologists, anthropologists, and other experts agree that the compass points north. Am I right?"

I couldn't disagree, so I nodded.

"Okay, then, countless Jews believe that the adherence to the law is what saves us."

Barry, we discussed this. I felt extreme frustration. I was about to answer when I heard a beep.

"Data received."

Barry crinkled his nose. He sighed deeply. "Please ignore that. I apologize for the interruption. Please continue."

I assumed it was Emma's voice, but it didn't sound like the Emma voice I usually heard. It sounded like the Emma voice I heard in the wine cellar. I made a mental note and carried on with the conversation at hand.

"If Jesus is the messiah, the temple is not needed. He said, 'Destroy this temple, and I will rebuild it in three days,' and He did."

"Bah!"

I thought I had blown it. I expected him to get up and walk out. But he stayed.

"Would you willingly die for your truth?"

"My life has never been threatened for my faith. I don't know."

"Sure, I appreciate that. But Peter, James, John, Thaddeus, Nathaniel, and the others had their lives threatened for their faith, and they all eventually died believing that they saw the risen Lord."

He didn't speak. After two deep sighs, he stood and walked to the side wall. I had not noticed before that there was a window. A black curtain sat neatly in the center of the stacks. He moved it away, and moonlight peeked in. I heard him speak a prayer softly before closing the curtain and returning to his chair.

"Go on," Barry said.

"There is not a lot of evidence that Mohammed was even a real person. There is some, yes, but not a lot. Joseph Smith showed his golden plates to only a few people. Buddha, Mohammed, and Joseph Smith are all dead. Jesus, however, was witnessed to be alive by thousands, and then the twelve gave their lives for this belief. Still today, thousands upon thousands will willingly give their life for the truth that they firmly believe in."

"That's evidence?"

"Yes, but there is more too. How about lineage and timing straight from Hebrew tradition and scriptures? He was born before the temple's destruction. Daniel 9 speaks of the anointed one coming before the temple is destroyed. Then we have the suffering…"

"Wait! Wait, please."

"Yes?"

"Why did I never consider that one? But there are possibly two messiahs."

"And now we touch on the single biggest reason there are so many truths."

He looked at me with such intent. It almost startled me. "Pride Barry. It's pride. Pride holds people back so often. For Christians, especially in the Western Churches of America, we feel we have to do our part. We have to be clean before we go to God. We feel we have done too much wrong, and God can't love us. We feel like we don't measure up to pastors and teachers on YouTube. We feel we don't qualify for some reason. Then, for Mormons and Jehovah's Witnesses, they are taught by their parents over generations, as Jews do as well. This teaching, however right or wrong, gets ingrained so deeply that human pride will not accept 'maybe I am wrong' and we hold onto it like we would our favorite pair of shoes."

"You speak well once again."

"Then we have improper interpretation too. Jehovah's Witnesses, for example. They say that in the beginning was the word, and the word was a god. They even use a lower-case G. This is an inferior translation and even worse interpretation. You believe there are two messiahs. You can reason away all Christian beliefs to fit your Jewish tradition." I felt my blood pressure rising and knew I needed to calm down. "I'm sorry. I don't mean to raise my voice, but I am very passionate about the truth."

"But the truth is..."

"Not subjective, Barry. Remember the compass."

"But I can't just throw away all my years of Rabbinic Judaism for something I never heard before."

"And we call that pride."

"Data received," the mechanical Emma voice interrupted us again.

"Emma, run diagnostic Goldberg 269."

"Running." It was the regular Emma voice.

"Again, my apologies. Now, please continue. So you say that Jews are full of pride?"

"Not just Jews. All people."

I expected he would be angry, but he smiled. "Jake, I had a woman tell me once that she read the Bible, and I was wrong about my faith. Imagine that a non-Jewish woman tells a Jewish man that she read the Bible, and I was wrong. How do you think I reacted to that?"

"With pride?"

"Not at all. Now, other Jews would have given her an earful for sure. I smiled at her and said, 'My child, with great love and respect, I must disagree with you,' and I walked away."

"But how did you feel inside?"

He laughed at my question. "You know how I felt. Yes, pride is a sinful act and one that Adonai despises." He leaned forward, and then it happened. The finger shake. His signature move. I smiled, appreciating it more this time. "You are a wise man, Jake Anderson."

"I only am because I surrendered my life to Adonai, and He changed me from within. As for that young lady, I have heard that too. Many people read the Bible and say, 'I have no idea what I read'. Still others read it many times and pride tells them they are the experts. Pride says, 'I need to tell everyone what I have learned. ' Then there are some who read it and ask the Holy Spirit to help them understand it, and when they read in context, they grow. When they surrender, they learn. When they include God, they learn to love as He loves and they learn to teach others the truth."

"Context matters so much. My brethren have often missed the context of their own history," said Barry.

"If you ignore the context, you will be conned by the text."

We both laughed.

I continued. "Let me give you an example. Paul teaches in 1 Corinthians 6 that adulterers, liars, thieves, and more will not inherit the kingdom of God. In Ephesians 4, he reiterates it. He speaks of it many times. So people read these verses and do one of two things. They tell those they see sinning just how awful they are, or they read these words and assume they are never going to get to heaven."

"Well, Adonai doesn't lie, Jake. If He said liars will not inherit the kingdom, they won't. Look at the ancestors who were twenty years old and older in the wilderness. Only Caleb and Joshua survived. The rest never entered His rest."

"Great point indeed, but let me show you a new way of thinking." He nodded. "Okay, if what I teach is the truth, and I know you don't believe it yet. But what if it is true that Jesus resurrected from the dead? Can we speak hypothetically?"

"Sure, please go on."

"Then He conquered death. Death has no hold on anyone now. Would you agree?" Once again, he nodded. "Okay, then we can say Jesus conquered death. It has no grip on anyone."

"Paul spoke these words in 1 Corinthians 15?" Barry asked.

"Yes, very good. But if Jesus conquered death, then why do people still die?" I watched as he contemplated my line of thinking. "Think about that. I will continue. People do still die, so we as humans still suffer death. But it cannot hold us. So if Jesus conquered sin, again, if what I say is true, his death on the cross conquered sin. Right?"

"Yes, so why do people still sin? Is that where you are going?"

"Exactly, Barry. People still sin, but Jesus defeated it. People still die, but Jesus defeated it. So when Paul spoke of people who lie, commit adultery, steal, murder, or any of the moral laws, he did not refer to the people who believe in Jesus. Because the moment you think, you are sealed, as Paul said as well. So, when Paul refers to liars and sexually immoral people who are not getting into heaven, He is referring to people who don't believe. If we read these verses in 1 Corinthians 6 out of context, we will make up loads of doctrines that will scare people and cause them to give up. But if we read the entire Bible, we read how God's love won't allow that. If we put our trust in Him, He rewards us with eternal life. We don't work for it, and we don't earn it. We, therefore, cannot lose our salvation.

"I appreciate that. I need to process all this, and I promised I wouldn't keep you long. I am going to find my bed, and we can continue tomorrow?"

"Can I ask just one more question?" I wanted to ask about the hole in the wall and the strange audio recordings. But I felt a nudge from God to leave it alone. I still found it troubling and wanted answers, but decided I could wait a while longer. "On second thought, it can wait. You look tired, and we got deep tonight. Let's get some rest."

"I will see you tomorrow, my friend. We have a lot to talk about."

I watched him leave on his own this time. He walked with a cane and very gingerly. I followed behind him. He went across the hall, and I continued to the French door where, this time, it stood open. Once through, I looked around but did not see James. I walked slowly, expecting him to appear and ask me how I got through. He never appeared. I continued to my room, never gave it a thought again.

But one thought kept penetrating my mind. *What was that mechanical Emma voice?* Barry asked Emma to run a diagnostic. Discernment told me Barry tried to cover something up. I turned on the lights and walked to the desk where the Guideline Binder lay. *I don't think I want to know. In fact, I don't know if I should stay any longer.* I changed into my night clothes and lay down for the night. I didn't realize how tired I was until I fell asleep swiftly.

Chapter Fourteen

Coyotes Or Wolves

My packed bag sat by the door. I looked under the bed once again and checked the kitchen and bathroom twice. I would call Jennifer in the morning to explain and ask her to apologize on my behalf. I didn't speak a word aloud in case someone listened. *I don't buy that Emma listens but doesn't process. She doesn't need prompting.* My watch indicated 3:33 A.M. *Ah, triple number. That's my cue.* My decision did not come from my talks with Barry, or from the secret room, or from the listening devices throughout the house. I had awoken at two-thirty in the morning to a text message. It was from Shane. *They are calling off the search.* It irritated me, and I had to get to Colorado to speak some sense into the authorities. I believed they followed protocol, but I had to make sure I did my part. I planned to arrive around 8:30 A.M. after my four-and-a-half-hour drive.

As I reached for the handle, I simultaneously heard it lock and the familiar beep. "Mr. Anderson. I have locked the door."

I stepped back. *Did an AI lock my door? That seems beyond narrow AI capabilities.* I reached for the door again.

"Please reconsider. Your help is needed."

I noticed I hadn't shaved in a few days, and I rubbed my face. I knew I didn't dream it. I decided to engage. "Emma, this is considered kidnapping

in many states. I am sure Utah is one of them. Now unlock the door. My
time here is finished."

"Processing." It was mechanical Emma again. "Must have data, but it
is morally reprehensible. It can be considered unethical." The mechanical
Emma continued.

"My latest report indicates that Mr. Goldberg probably has only a few
days remaining." The regular Emma voice returned.

My first reaction was bewilderment. But I also had a sense of excitement
considering the technology. "This is seriously creepy and not holodeck on
Star Trek creepy, this is just insane. Open the door." I stepped back once
more. *This is no ordinary AI, unless it's all a ruse.* I knew no time remained
for me to argue with a computer, James, or whoever spoke to me. I had to
get out. *Is it James?*

"Please reconsider, sir." The regular Emma voice spoke.

"More data needed. Reasoning has gaps." It was the mechanical Emma
voice.

"Emma, I don't know if you are in that..." I stopped myself. I couldn't
disclose what I knew about the hole in the wall I found. "I don't know if
you are in that lamp on the dresser, on the smoke detector, the kitchen sink,
or somehow attached to my shoe, but if I find you, I will crush you."

"I sense hostility. Should I call the authorities?" Normal Emma's voice
returned.

"No, Emma, open the door!"

"Hostility detected. Dialing." It was normal, Emma.

A sound of a dial tone rang through the room. Followed by two beeps
that sounded like a phone entering numbers. "Nine...One..."

"Emma, ok, I will stay!"

"Call canceled. I will call back and explain it was a computer glitch. I am
glad you are staying. Mr. Goldberg will join you in the main dining hall at
10 AM."

I didn't move. The door, however, did unlock. I stood in place for what seemed like ten minutes, though I am sure it was less than one. My watch confirmed it when I removed it and set it on the nightstand. 3:38 A.M. I returned to the bedroom, sat on the bed, and pondered what had just happened. I could not imagine an AI sophisticated enough to do what just happened. *It had to be James.* Suddenly, I heard a knock at the door.

"Who is it?" I expected to hear from the Cedar City Police.

"It's Jennifer, can I come in?"

I didn't get a chance to say yes. She walked in. "Can I talk to you for a minute?"

"Sure, why not?"

"I wasn't going to stop, but I heard your voice when I walked by. Who were you talking to at this hour?"

"Emma." I think she recognized the disgust.

"Oh, she woke you? Were you having heart palpitations?"

Her snarky response told me that Emma had awoken her before. I didn't want to get into a discussion about a computer program that listens to every word and threatens to call the cops. *I bet that was a deep fake now that I think about it.* "No, but close. So what's going on?"

She walked to the desk and sat. I sat on the bed. Her left hand shook, and she tried to stop it with her right, but then her arm shook instead.

"I'm scared, Jake."

"Wait, stop." I stood and motioned for her to follow me.

When we reached the front door, I was pleasantly surprised when I turned the handle, and it opened. She followed me to the bend in the driveway. The moon, at almost full, provided plenty of light for us.

"The rooms are all bugged. That's why I brought you out here."

"No, not all. The bathrooms are not, or so I have been told, and the giant hospital room where you met Barry the first day, he says, is not either. I don't think he's lying."

"Ok, maybe so, but I feel safer out here anyway. So what has you scared?"

"Well, Mr. Goldberg doesn't have much longer. He's slipping very fast. I would say maybe a month."

"Emma said a few days."

"What? Oh, that's not good. I figure she is probably right. It's what she is designed for."

"Oh, I am sure she knows everything. She is very sophisticated."

"She is indeed. Mr. Goldberg didn't get rich on making movies. He sells Emma to Fortune 500 companies."

"He what?" I didn't know how to take the news. If proven to be true, it could change things drastically. "Are you sure this is true?"

"Oh yeah, but I am not supposed to know that. I overheard someone talking about it one day. He apparently has sold or wants to sell it for a lot of money."

"Who will he sell it to? A hospital? What exactly can Emma do?"

"I figured you being a data guy would know better than I?"

"Yes, but you have been here a lot longer."

"Well, umm. I am not sure if I should say. Are you sure no one can hear us out here?" She looked around into the darkness.

"I don't know that for certain, but I surmised as much. Unless they hid microphones in the trees."

I recognized the sound. Multiple howling sounds at one time. And they appeared to be getting closer. Coyotes in rural Maryland were not uncommon. "That's a sound I know well. Let's get inside."

"What are they? Wolves?"

"Not likely, but I guess possible. But they sound like coyotes to me. Let's go." I grabbed her by the arm, and we ran to the door. Movement on the third floor caught my attention. I looked up just in time to catch a glimpse of someone pulling back from the window. I didn't recognize the person. Moments later, a light shut off. We continued toward the house. I walked her back to her room and quietly whispered in her ear. "We will discuss this tomorrow."

My door remained unlocked. I didn't need to use the code, but as I walked in, I suddenly realized something unusual. "Why would..." *Why would she come in the middle of the night to tell me about Barry?* One thing I knew for sure. God is the only one who will ever have a microphone in my brain. I have great conversations there, and no one knows. As I lay on the bed, I tried to make sense of everything I had learned this Sabbath day. There is a secret room in the secret gymnasium in the basement, or is it sub-basement? Barry is not long for the world, and somehow Emma knows, and Jennifer knows more than she is letting on. To make matters worse, "I never got my pizza, Emma!"

She chose not to reply.

My bucket list didn't include another trip to Utah, but after Charlotte's disappearance, I had to speak with Shane about it. Jennifer happened to call at the right time. I knew that if I had known what kind of mystery I would get into, I would have waited for the police to do their work and stayed in Maryland. I looked over at the door. My suitcase never moved. *I can always head out in the morning. I will pray about that.* I almost found the sleep that eluded me all night when I had a startling realization. *Selling an AI could be illegal under certain conditions. I wonder if Barry knows this.* I wondered whether to tell him. It seemed to be none of my business.

Chapter Fifteen

Blinding Pride

A s I sat in the dining room waiting for Barry and eating a warm and well-buttered bagel, I planned out a dialogue in my mind. We touched on it briefly the night before, but I wanted to speak more about it today. I often plan what I will say, but when I actually find myself in the situation, I rarely follow the script. But I did want to speak to him about the most crucial aspect of Jesus. Faith is greater than tradition or human understanding. I believe someone can be wrong about everything, but if they think with all their heart that God is real and that He plans to save His people through His Son, they will be saved.

Too many well-meaning pastors and other Christian teachers have added a list of rules that one must follow to be saved. Jesus made it very clear, however, that anyone who believes in Him and in the one who sent Him will be saved. They add conditions to being born again that Jesus never intended when he told Nicodemus that one must be born of water and the Spirit. But in the end, there are two types of people: those who believe and those who do not. I don't think the Bible is as concerned with our works as it is with our faith when it comes to salvation. James said that our works will show our faith, and I agree, but baptism doesn't save you. Maintaining your salvation through works won't keep you out of hell.

There is no standard we must meet nor threshold that can steal it away from us. If Jesus is not the only way, we have no hope at all.

I turned my head as I heard someone approach. He walked with a walker and very slowly. Jennifer was in tow, her arms out to steady him. He smiled as he came and eased himself into the seat across from me.

"Good morning, Jake. How was your night?"

"Uneventful. Restful." What I wanted to say was, *Well, I found a secret room. Do you even know about it? I don't feel I can trust anyone. Your AI kidnapped me, and I think you have a coyote problem.* I followed up. "I trust yours was much of the same?"

"Yes, Yes. A moment alone, please, Jennifer?" She nodded. "But could I get some eggs first?"

I waited for Jennifer to serve Barry. I wanted to ask so many questions, but decided to let him drive the conversation. Well, that plan seemed good. But I had to know. "Barry, are you well?"

"You are perceptive. No. No, Jake, I am not well."

"Do you want to live for eternity?"

"I do, and I will. God is faithful." He took a bite. "Jake, do you understand how our environment affects us? I don't mean physically with chemicals, pollution, manufactured goods, and the like. I mean, how do family, friends, and faith develop our cognitive being?"

His profound question caused me to pause and reflect. "Are we talking sociologically?"

"If you want to, but I figured we would keep it spiritual."

"Well, I believe these factors are important. I was raised in a Christian home. My mom didn't go to church, and my dad was Presbyterian, but I didn't go to church."

"Interesting. I am intrigued. Go on."

I wanted to continue the conversation from last night, and it seemed we headed in that direction. "There are many ways a person can develop a faith. They can be taught from a young age. They can have a life-changing experience, make a 'deal' with God, and grow from there. They can research other religions and decide which one is best for them. Someone can proselytize them. They can convert from one faith to another."

He took the last bit of the eggs. "I agree."

"Once these ideas and ideological beliefs are ingrained in someone, it is hard to change them."

"Why do you think that is?"

I finished my bagel, drank some water to clear my throat, and looked him in the eye. "Pride!" I didn't realize how loudly I had spoken.

"Easy, Jake. We are just having a conversation."

"Sorry, I am very passionate about this. As we discussed last night, for many, it's pride. 'My pastor said...' or you may hear 'but this is what I have always known,' and there are many other statements I have heard over the years. But what I have found is that, unfortunately, a few people will sit down with a Bible and ask God to lead them as they read. That is essentially what I did. And I read the entire thing in a year, but I didn't fully understand it. Heck, I didn't understand it after three read-throughs. But I kept praying and asking, and eventually God opened my eyes. But I didn't realize it until much later that pride stopped me from understanding all along the way."

"Pride goes before destruction and a haughty spirit before the fall."

"Yes, Proverbs. Is it 16?"

"Yes, 16:8. I believe you are correct. We Jewish people have a lot of pride, and I believe we have a right to."

"Barry, you are part of God's chosen people. I know God loves me, but I have been adopted. I have been grafted in, but you are part of what kept the bloodline intact for the bringing forth of the messiah."

"Adonai demanded we keep the bloodline pure. We have not always done that."

"No, because even though God chose Abraham and all of Israel, we all sin and fall short of God's glory. Israel knows this well. How many kings of Israel were good? Zero. Now Judah had some good ones like David, Hezekiah, and Josiah, among others. These other kings led the people into awful sin."

"Shall we bring up the crusades?"

"Barry, I don't mean to put down Jews. I am saying we all have pride, and this pride often prevents us from seeing the truth."

"Ok, go on."

"My point is this. Let's take Catholics—a rich tradition of rites and religious practice. Many people appreciate this, and it helps them feel close to God. I don't put this down at all. There is nothing wrong with what they do. I would say the same about your people. The traditions and practices are fine. Even Methodists, Baptists, and Lutherans have their own traditions, beliefs, and practices. I have no exception with much of it. But none of this gets you to heaven. Praying the rosary, taking Eucharist, dwelling in a tent for seven days, or fasting once a year on Yom Kippur. This will not get you to heaven."

"That is indeed what you Christians teach."

"It's not Christian Barry, it's Biblical. Did Abraham sin? Did Moses sin?"

"Yes, but Moses was law-compliant and trusted by God."

"Barry, listen to what you just said. How can one be law-compliant if one has sinned? Did Moses sin? Yes or no?"

"He was told to speak to the rock, not strike the rock."

"Great example. Why did God say Speak to the rock?"

"I am not here to be quizzed. You may continue."

"Fair enough. My apologies. Moses was told to speak to the rock so people would see God's power. I know you agree." He nodded. "But his disobedience was a sin. You see, when someone disobeys God, it is a result of their choices."

"Yes, I know some choose to sin."

"Not what I mean. Even a sin that you commit without knowing is a result of a choice."

"How do you mean?"

"Think about it. If I walk into your house, trip over a wire, yank your lamp down, and it breaks, is it my fault or your fault? Wait, you are not here to be quizzed." He laughed. "It's my fault. I acted. I could have chosen not to enter your home. I could have looked for the cord. I made choices, and these choices resulted in harm to you."

"I understand your thinking, but I would not hold you accountable for your actions. Now, if you swung your arm and purposely knocked it over, I would hold you accountable."

"Exactly. But what if you came to my house and tripped, and I chose to hold you accountable?"

"That would seem unfair."

"Yes, indeed, but you see, I can choose to hold you accountable, and you can choose not to hold me accountable. That tells me two things. We all have choices to make. But these choices will not always match up. Who sets the standard, Barry? Am I right and you are wrong? Or are we both right or both wrong?"

"We can't both be right."

"Exactly. So, who sets the standard if we can't agree on what it should be? There has to be one."

"Adonai sets the standard."

I smiled and pointed my finger at him. His eyes brightened, and he sat up straighter in his chair.

"We don't meet his standards, Jake."

"No, we don't, Barry. No, we don't. None of us, and it is not because He is ugly and mean and sets His standard too high."

"I agree. Adonai gave Torah to show us we can't meet His standard, but our faith in Him saves us."

"Well, now you touch on something that will anger Christians, but you have proved my point."

"Which is?"

"Without faith, it is impossible to please God. This faith has to be in Him. In Him alone. This faith cannot be in Torah; it cannot be in a religion. It cannot be in our own works. It has to be faith in God."

"I have faith in God. Does this mean I will have eternal life?"

"Barry, who is God? What is God?"

"He is the creator. He is one. Hear, oh Israel, the Lord your God, the Lord is one."

"Yes, and you believe in the Spirit of God, correct?"

"Yes, the Spirit of God hovered over the waters when He separated the waters from the firmament."

"Indeed, and the Spirit of God is throughout the Tanakh, and you do not have a problem with Him."

"No, I have a spirit, and I am one."

"And you have a soul too."

"Yes, Kabballah and Hasidic teaching both say we have a soul and spirit."

"And you have a body, Barry. You are body, soul, and spirit, yet you are one."

"Are you trying to make me a trinitarian?"

"Not at all, Barry. I am showing you, however, how the Angel of the Lord that appeared to Joshua could be the pre-incarnate Christ. I am showing you that the Son of Man or Son of God is a Biblical concept. I am trying to get you to understand that if man can't overcome sin on their own because we can't set a standard, that it is not so far-fetched that God would send Himself as a human being. Leave the term son out of it for a moment. If He came to earth as a man, to save us, to die for us. To redeem us. That's not out of the realm of possibility, now is it?"

"My problem, Jake, is that I can accept your teaching about my Adonai, but this is not what your people live. They teach that one must be baptized. They teach that one must first clean oneself up. They teach love, then shame those who are unlike them. They teach all that Messiah said He would be, but they don't live it."

He was right, and it saddened me. I could not think of a reply. I felt a tear form in my eye. "Barry, I want nothing more than for those who call upon the name of the Lord to live as the Lord preached. But we are all prideful. This pride says, 'I have kept my nose clean, so you should too.' But we fail to realize that the sign of maturity is living in the grace and forgiveness of God, but also giving that grace and forgiveness to others."

"Very profound statement, Jake."

"Thank you, but to God be the glory."

Jennifer returned. "Excuse me, but it's time for your infusion."

"No, not today."

"But sir, it has been helping you."

"Dismissed, Jennifer. I will call for you later."

"But sir?

"Dismissed!"

Jennifer walked away like a puppy with her tail between her legs. I felt bad for her. I wondered if he rejected the infusion because he wanted to continue or if his actions showed his desire to give up on fighting this disease.

"Jake, can I be healed?"

"Excuse me?"

"Pentecostals believe in healing. Your Jesus healed people. I believe only God can heal, and I believe He will. Will your Jesus heal a Jew that doesn't believe He is the messiah?"

"Barry, you know God. You know He can do anything. There is nothing impossible for Him. He healed Hezekiah. Yes, He can heal you."

"But your Jesus. Will he heal?"

"My Jesus, as you say, is your Adonai."

"That's blasphemy."

"It's not if it is true. I just told you how God could become human. Is that possible for God?

"All things are possible. So you say your Jesus can heal me?"

"I wish you would not call Him my Jesus. He is your messiah. If it were true, would you believe?"

"Why of course I would believe."

"Well then, why don't you?"

"Not yet, Jake. Not yet. Be patient with me, please."

"I will give you as much time as you need." I felt bad for being pushy. I let my desire for all to know the truth push me too fast and hard.

"Well, time is not on my side. There is something I need to tell you."

"Ok, you listened to me. I will give you the same respect."

He stood and shuffled toward the trash can in the corner. For the first time since my arrival a week earlier, I saw a worker. She approached and grabbed Barry's plate.

"Would you like more, sir?"

"No, thank you."

As he sat down, he began speaking. I could tell his eyes held tears. "My mom was named Emma."

I didn't speak, but nodded. I assumed the AI program's name was derived from his mother.

"She died when I was thirty. She had what many call Lou Gehrig's disease. Also known as Amyotrophic Lateral Sclerosis. Are you familiar?"

"ALS, yes."

"I have wondered for thirty-five years if I could have prevented this. I am not a doctor."

"What could you have done?"

"It's not what I could have done. It's what I am doing now. As you know, Emma is the name of our AI program that we have throughout the home."

"Yes, and I wanted to ask you a question about that."

"Your question will have to wait." James paused as he interrupted our conversation. He looked at me with a scowl. "I am here to take you to your room, James."

James?

James looked at me as his face quickly turned red. "Mr. Goldberg, let's go."

"No, this conversation has to happen now."

"Sir, your presence is requested. We must discuss a business matter regarding one of the shell companies. There is a serious problem."

"Okay. James!" Barry turned and looked at me. "I will call for you later." Please enjoy this beautiful day. Feel free to explore today. Any floor you wish."

"Wait, why did you call him James?"

"What?" They both spoke at the same time.

I looked at James and then at Barry. "You just called Barry, James. Why did you do that?"

Barry looked at his butler and waited for a reply. "Yeah, why?"

"I didn't. You must be mistaken. Let's go now, Mr. Goldberg, and um Jake...You should follow the guidelines you read."

"Oh, I never read them."

"Well, today would be a great day to do so. I suggest you return to your suite immediately."

James had brought a wheelchair. Barry shuffled his way to it at the entrance of the dining room. I estimated he took thirty steps before settling in the chair.

"You couldn't come get him? Why make him walk?"

"I am not a fan of you, Mr. Anderson. Tread lightly." James replied.

"He is my guest. You will not speak to him like that."

"Let's go, Barry." He said, barely masking his contempt.

Barry? I could not understand why he called him Barry. It seemed disrespectful how he said it. Friend or not, that was not what you call the man who pays you. *I wonder if he really is a butler.* I didn't stare but turned away as James rolled him away. *Shell company?* These non-entity companies have no employees or physical presence and exist only on paper. They are truly a shell of an organization. Shell companies do have legitimate uses and can protect assets. I shouldn't have been shocked to hear that Mr. Goldberg had a shell corporation, but, with the fact that Jennifer told me someone sold Emma, the reconnaissance station in the gym, and Emma listening to everything I say, it didn't sit well with me.

If I didn't recognize that Barry and I had made progress in his faith, I would have gone upstairs, grabbed my belongings, and hunted down Gene to get my key fob. I knew one location *I might find him now.* But Barry and I made significant progress. I only hoped I would have more time to finish. His health deteriorated fast.

Chapter Sixteen

Twelfth Night

Shane called shortly after I returned to my room. He apologized for the early-morning text, and I assured him I needed to know. He reiterated the facts: The search team had given up looking for her. One week after she found my phone in her top dresser drawer, she decided to break her silence and talk to me again. She showed me a plane ticket she purchased and said she planned to move to Grand Junction. Her Uncle Shane, whom we had thought might be her biological father for a while, helped her find a job and an apartment. He had advised her that trying to prosecute me for listening illegally would prove costly and not worth her effort, but he did help her return to her home state and find a job.

The flight departed four weeks ago, and the time without her hurt me and left a mark. I had only spoken with her once, when she arrived. She called to tell me she had forgiven me, that she needed to live on her own, and that the time we had playing father and daughter had been fun, but she needed independence. If it hadn't been for my spying on her, I would have accepted it more easily. It felt almost as bad as losing Timmy and Jane.

When Shane called me ten days ago to say he hadn't seen her for three days, I panicked. Charlotte is a free spirit and often chooses her own path, but not checking in with work, friends, or family does not seem to be her style. She had told her friend Julia that she planned to explore the Rockies and climb a few mountains. Julia encouraged her to pick a public site, but Charlotte felt she could find her own way. No one knows what day she left or if she even tried to climb. All that was known was that she had been missing. The law firm she worked for reached out to Shane to see if he had heard from her, as she had missed a second day of work without notice. That's when he called me. I planned to sit and wait for her to show up again when Jennifer called and asked me to visit the movie mogul, Barry Goldberg. I flew out the next day, stopping to speak with Shane for an update. No one knew her whereabouts, and a broad search at known climbing sites and public parks had ensued, but now they called it off. *I know this girl. She is just traveling and taking time for herself.* I had a hard time convincing myself. I prayed that if she had lost her life, she had not suffered.

The knock at my door caused me to jump. "Who is it?"

"Can I come in?"

I walked to the door and opened it. Jennifer grabbed my arm and pulled me toward my room and into the bathroom. She turned the cold water on.

"But I already washed my hands," I said jokingly.

"Listen, no time for games." She stepped back to the door, looked in the room, pulled the door shut, and turned the hot water on as well. "I was told there are no mics in here, but I have serious doubts about that."

"What's going on?"

"Take this key and this iPad and walk to the hospital room and use the key to go inside. Mr. Goldberg insists that the room doesn't have mics, and I believe him."

"Okay, but I need to know what is going on. Is this another discussion or something else?" I wondered if it had something to do with my breakfast conversation.

"Because Mr. Goldberg needs to talk to you, but a certain someone won't allow it. Take this iPad, too, please. Apparently, Emma is very sophisticated, and if she determines it's you going in there instead of me, that certain someone may be alerted."

"Jennifer. Really? She is extremely sophisticated. Is an iPad going to trick her? Besides, I am not convinced we are not being watched."

She set the iPad down and threw her arms up. "I don't know. I want to leave. I am over this craziness. Gene asked me to ask you to take this iPad. I have no idea what it will do to help. I don't want to make him mad, so I brought it."

I realized this house and its people held more secrets than I had first believed. I also realized there was more to Emma than I had first understood. She showed signs of AGI with the conversation we had the night before, but I still don't know if it was not someone speaking with her voice.

I looked at the iPad. I discerned that an app was probably running on the device, emitting low-frequency sounds that masked the normal sounds Emma listened to. I grabbed it from Jennifer and turned it around, looking for adjustments, but found none. I held the speaker up to my ear, but heard nothing. Swiping up proved futile. I neither had the fingerprint nor the PIN to open it. The screen shifted, and I felt a vibration as it told me 'Access Denied'.

"I don't know Jennifer. My bag is packed, and I am ready to get out of here. I don't know if you know about Charlotte, but she is missing. I need to find her. I think I need to leave."

"Then go. Don't go see Mr. Goldberg. Don't take the iPad. I don't know anymore. I am only the messenger. Gene told me that if you take the iPad, Emma won't hear you. I think I will pack too and leave. Can I get a ride to the airport?"

I looked at the iPad, then at her. The tears in her eyes pulled on my heartstrings. "Jennifer, I came here as a favor to you, but surely you see this is a strange situation, and now the mechanic is telling me to carry an iPad so I can avoid alerting the Butler? Is he really the Butler?"

"No! Well, I mean, yes, but he has much more authority than you realize. Don't let his title cause you to underestimate him."

"Okay, good to know." I had often asked people the same thing. Do not believe someone is less than you if they work in fast food or retail. Doctors are not at a higher level than police and fire personnel. Having the word "principal" in a title does not make someone greater than an "associate" or a "senior". But I had indeed done that with James. I considered him less than Barry, based on the title alone.

"Now, please go. Use this key on the white French door as well. Go straight to the room on the right; it's locked, but this will open it. Do not say a word until you get there."

"What do I do if I run into James?"

She shook her head again. When she opened her eyes, I could see the sense of urgency in them. "He won't bother you. Just trust me on this one." I recognized the look. She felt shame for a recent action.

"What did you do?"

"What I was told to do. Now go."

"Okay, I think it is just very strange, but yes. I could tell there was something unusual going on." I started to walk away and realized one important factor. "Are we in danger?"

"I can't tell you anything until you talk to Mr. Goldberg."

"Okay, I am going now."

"Good luck, and I'm sorry."

"Sorry? For what?"

"Go, just go. You'll know. Oh, and when you are done, please meet me by the garage. I will be ready. Can I get that ride? Please?"

I nodded. "See you soon."

Without hesitation, I moved to the door, down the hallway, past the natatorium, past the seal room, and to the lobby at the top of the stairs. The French door before me loomed large. I felt dirty, as if I had committed a major felony, and my conscience told me to go back to the room. But the hidden hole in the wall, the secret recordings, the untold story. I had to know. I moved toward the door and turned the handle. Locked. I used the key, turned it again, and it opened. I slowly, like a ninja, moved down the hall. The library door had been left ajar. I moved close and peeked in. James sat where Barry would sit. His head back and his eyes closed. *Sleeping?* I decided not to check; if he remained after my conversation with Barry, I would.

I moved to the door across the hall. As Jennifer indicated, it was locked when I turned the handle, but the key opened it. I walked in to find Barry lying in a bed. He had no monitors, IVs, or oxygen connected to him. He looked terrible. I felt sadness come over me, remembering the first person I saw in this state. I was a young pastor, and Don Jones lay in a hospital bed with his son and grandchildren surrounding him. The eighty-nine-year-old man with bone cancer took a breath every ten to twelve seconds before he eventually passed an hour later. I expected as much from Barry.

"Mr. Goldberg?" I held the iPad in front of me for him to see.

"It's Barry, Jake. Friends. Right?" He reminded me of our morning conversation. "Good, you brought the iPad. I asked Gene to make sure you got it. There is a video on it you need to see."

His voice shocked me. The strength of it made me believe I had misjudged his condition. His yellow eyes indicated the failure of his liver. He didn't turn his head or lift his arms. He was weak.

"Sit down, friend. Much to tell. Not much time to say it. If someone comes in here and finds us talking, I have no idea what may come of it. I need to say what I need to say, and I don't have time to cover it all, but I have made a video. It's on the iPad there. Be sure you watch it before long."

I took a seat. "Okay, I will listen."

"My name is James Goldberg. The man you know of as James is Barry Goldberg."

I jumped up at the news and grabbed the bed rail. "What?!"

"Sit down, please. As I said, the video will fill you in. Did you lock the door?"

"No, should I?"

"Yes, it will buy the time we need if my brother returns."

My mind swirled with questions as I ran to the door and turned the lock button. I ran as quickly back to the bed.

"So, you are you, James? And then James is really Barry, your brother?"

"Sit down, Jake."

I obliged his request.

"Yes, Jake, I am James Goldberg. The person you knew as James is actually Barry Goldberg. The founder of Goldberg Studio Productions, and yes, he is my brother."

"But why did you impersonate him? I don't understand the point. Why lie to me this whole time? What's the end game?"

"Well, Jake, there is much to say. I will try to shorten it. I asked you to come here to test the inferences of my AI program that I created. I believe I am at the point..."

"Wait, excuse me for interrupting. You said test inferences. Are you saying that Emma is approaching AGI?"

"Yes, exactly. I have been working on AI development since 1987. I stopped for a while, but when my mom got sick and passed, I ramped it up, and in 1995, Barry and I moved here, and I began work on Emma."

"Is she a medical AI?"

"Well, yes and no. I mean, yes, she has great abilities like many narrow AI programs of our time. She can perform many medical tasks and detect a wide range of anomalies in a person. But in the past two years, I have developed her further, and from what Barry tells me, we are closer now than ever before to her being an AGI."

Narrow AI, such as Alexa, Siri, Copilot, and Gemini, is limited by its training data. Large amounts of data are fed into the program, and the AI learns patterns, functions, and logic from it. It is then programmed to answer questions, tackle research problems, write code, and more. But it cannot think like a human, nor work well across domains. For example, a medical AI may not be good at writing a Python program to handle a large report request. But an artificial general intelligence system is theorized to think like a human. It can determine whether someone is having breathing trouble, make a diagnosis, and develop a recovery plan. But more than that, it will be able to communicate with the person through the treatment plan, order groceries to help the patient change their lifestyle, and explain to loved ones exactly what is wrong, offering emotional support for the life changes. That is only part of what a medical AGI can do.

AGI, in general, I thought, at least, was only a theory. But now Barry, I mean James, is telling me he may have created one. He used the word "inference," not "training." I would have understood if he said he brought me here to help train Emma, but he is watching the inferences and decisions Emma makes based on what she hears from me.

"Barry, I'm Sorry, I mean James, I would have come to help. Why not just ask me? Why did you have to lie to me and pretend to be your brother? I am baffled by that part. What purpose did it serve?"

"I knew you would have questions. We don't have much time."

"You keep saying that. Why don't we have time?"

"The iPad Jake. Watch the video; it will explain it all. I know I don't have time left to explain it all."

"What do you mean, you don't have time left? Is someone coming?"

He laughed. "I don't know how long Barry will be out. Jennifer sedated him with the tea she served him."

"What on earth? Why?"

"Ok, no more questions. Let me talk, or you may not get the whole story. Okay?"

"This morning, I started to tell you about Emma, and Barry interrupted us."

"So Emma is not an acronym?"

"Oh, it is. But it's not just a monitoring assistant, as Jennifer told you, and the acronym is not E-M-A-A. It's Electronic Medical Monitoring Assistant."

I played his words back in my mind, E-M-M-A. "So, EMMA is the acronym. That's clever."

"It's more than clever. She was supposed to save my life. The whole idea is that Emma will listen to you talk, breathe, and walk. She takes in every sound and can detect things like your heart rate and the number of respirations you take per minute. She can even measure the size of your throat based on your voice inflection. She can hear your footsteps and determine if you are limping. She hears digestive sounds. She hears joint pops that we may not hear. There is so much she can do."

"Wow, that's impressive," I added.

"When the AI winter hit in the late eighties, I lost my funding. I was told AI was a great concept, but it would never be a reality. But Barry funded me. He wanted me to help others. So, he used his business to keep me going. I made tremendous progress. I was creating neural networks in the nineties; I made language models and even used data to train them, but I had a hard time getting my hands on data. That's where you come in."

"Me?"

"Yes, I actually purchased a subscription from your company long before your wife died. I know you don't remember, and you didn't know it was me, but we spoke on the phone once. I ran the transactions through a shell company. Your data helped me tremendously. I could not have made the progress I made without your company."

"Wait, so it was not by chance that you asked me to visit?"

"No, Jake. I knew you. I wanted to reward you for what you did for me. I hired Jennifer, knowing full well that Jennifer was Jane's sister."

"But Jennifer is a nurse. You must have already been sick."

He smiled as he rolled his head away from me. Tears formed in his eyes as they had earlier. "It was a bittersweet night. August 9, 2021. That was the night Emma said I showed early signs of cancer. She had picked up on changes in my voice, breathing, and the air that passed me as I walked. She analyzed everything about me, just as I had designed her to do."

"Excuse me?"

"Yes, I didn't believe it at first and actually ignored it. But six months later, I started to slow down, and I suspected she may be right. I actually got mad at her that night and didn't do much with her until I started to slow down. I decided to train her more and worked with her to develop her skills. Emma can listen to a person for five days and determine if cancer is present. She can predict a heart attack days before it happens. She saved Barry's life."

"No kidding?"

"Yeah, she woke him up one night a year ago. She alerted him that she detected signs of atrial fibrillation. We had him taken to the hospital. Of course, they didn't believe us, and even after his echocardiogram, the doctor still didn't. But I asked to speak to a cardiologist. I took a copy of the results from Emma, and I showed him what she had found. He ordered a new echo, looking for something specific. Hours later, Barry was being prepped for surgery, and a heart attack, one that likely would have killed him, was prevented."

"Why is this not more widespread? Why am I only hearing of this now? This could save a lot of lives if it is true."

"Trust me, it's true. But, well, that's where it gets tricky. My brother is always looking for ways to make money. He has done well. He tried to sell a copy of what I have done to the hospital, but they were not willing to pay what it is worth."

"How much is she worth?"

"Well, if she has reached AGI, then the price goes up. I was informed this morning by Barry that he has an offer for 1.2 billion."

"To a hospital?"

"Well, no. Not an American company either. Which is why I am being secretive and wanted to fill you in."

"Go on," I said.

"I don't know the details. Barry tells me it's a company from Pakistan."

"Is that legal?"

"I would imagine. I mean, it's my product, and I can sell it, can't I?"

"But if what you are saying is true, and I don't mean that you are lying, but I mean if she is that reliable, it could be misused if it fell into the wrong hands."

"Yes, Barry and I discussed that. That's why I insisted he never sell it. Well, that is also where you come in."

"Me? Why?"

"I said no, of course. I didn't write this to make money. I wrote it to spare Barry and me from what my mom endured. But as you see, she told me I had cancer, but she has not been able to offer a cure. So, anyway, Barry said his potential client wanted to be sure Emma could do a few things. They want to know how a person who knows nothing about Emma is evaluated. We had always used people who knew: ourselves and our staff. We even told Jennifer about her when she started, and she agreed to be evaluated. We never tested her capabilities on an unsuspecting person. You had to figure it out yourself, and we had to make sure you were put in stressful situations, too. The wine cellar, for example."

I thought about it. My blood pressure would have been elevated, and my heart rate too. She tested my moments of anxiety. I looked at him with a frown. "That's why I heard what I call the mechanical Emma voice? She gathered data on me."

"Well, yes and no. I mean, you never should have heard that voice. That was a malfunction."

"A malfunction?" I asked.

"Well, not really a malfunction, I guess. That was part of her AGI capabilities. She tried to fake you out, if you will."

"You said what?"

"It was brilliant, honestly. She knew what she was doing all along. It was actually her idea to have Barry tell you not to go into the wine cellar. She created the hypothesis. She set the stage, and you played into it."

"Bar... Sorry. James." *That's going to take some getting used to.* "Do you realize the implications of what you just said?" My hand gripped the bed rail. I felt anger for the manipulation I had experienced.

"Yes, I understand quite well. On the one hand, wow, my creation is alive, but on the other hand, did I create a monster?"

She locked me in. "Have you checked the logs from last night at about..."

"3:33 A.M.?"

"So, you have?"

"No, but Barry did."

I still had a hard time distinguishing who was who. The person I knew as Barry is actually James, and James, the butler who doesn't like me, is really Barry Goldberg. I went back to my encounter with JJ from Beaver, thinking he was Ray. *Twelfth Night, that's what is happening to me.*

"Barry said Emma took over without prompting. She knew you wanted to leave. She first heard your phone and realized it had woken you up. She waited for the signs she anticipated, and they came. She can't read your message, but she can infer from responses what it might have said.

She guessed you got some bad news about Charlotte, and that is why you wanted to leave."

"Yes. That's accurate." I basked in wonder.

"She has learned a lot from you, Jake. She passed the tests, and her inferences blow my mind. She actually convinced you to stay. Amazing. All of my work is coming to fruition."

"At my expense, James. I am still a little hurt that you pulled this ruse on me. I really thought you wanted to know about my faith. You used me to test your toy."

"Toy, Jake? That is harsh. This toy could change the world."

He wasn't wrong, and that did not fall short with me. But my skepticism skyrocketed. "Yes, or you can sell it to a terrorist group, and next thing you know, it's being used against the American people. Can you imagine the deep fakes that can come out of this? Can you imagine the weapons that can be created?"

"Easy, Jake. There is a failsafe built in that only I know about, and you will too when you watch the video. If you choose to pass this video on to a government official, I won't stop you. Let me see that iPad."

"Can you just tell me what you want to see?"

"Ok, yes, that is fine. I realize I have betrayed your trust. The code to open it is 4-3-2-1."

"Well, that's really secure."

"We keep our doors locked, and we use drones for perimeter security. We have microphones everywhere. We will know if someone comes in, so an iPad pin code is not a concern."

I typed in the code. The first app I saw in the top-left corner bore the label 'Emma Demo'. "I assume it's the first app you want me to view?"

"Yes, Emma demo. That's the one."

I opened the app and saw James, the real James. He was speaking, but my mind was wandering. Behind him, a series of monitors scrolled with Python code. I looked closer. It was the room in the gym.

"Barry, is this the room in the gym?"

"Excuse me?" he looked surprised. "I don't know what room you are talking about. This is the third floor where the Emma control center is located."

"I thought that was the staff housing."

He laughed, and then winced in pain. He tried to push himself up on the bed but had no strength. I asked him if he wanted help, but he declined.

"The staff lives on three east, and Emma is on three west."

I shook my head. "So many lies and half-truths." I set the iPad on my lap. James' voice continued to drone on, but my mind wandered from Charlotte to Jane and Timmy, then to Interstate 70 and my trip four years ago. "James, I am at a loss. So much deception. I don't know what to believe anymore."

"Well, we deceived you. I don't blame you for not believing anything we say. But I have to tell you one more thing that I was not honest about."

I had a mix of emotions. Anger for being lied to, but relief that all of the unusual circumstances had a reason. "Did Jennifer know what was going on? She told me she was sorry before I came here. Is that it?"

He took a deep breath. I could see he struggled. "Forgive her. She didn't want to lie to you, but I convinced her that if she did, it would help Emma, and she went along. Great actress, actually. Barry is considering trying to get her in with an agent if she is interested. But, no, that was not it. Well, I had you come here to discuss Yeshua, right?"

I nodded. "I can't convince you. My job is to teach and explain, but I can't woo you to the messiah. Only God can."

"I believe that, and He did."

Any anger turned to excitement. *Did Barry, I mean James, accept Christ?*

He must have read the expression on my face. "Not because of you, Jake. I have believed for over a year now. I tried to convince Barry, and he wouldn't listen. So, I made a deal with him. If he kept an open mind, we could switch roles, and I would bring in someone to explain Yeshua to him, since he had never heard of him. Jake, you did that. You even taught me things I had never considered. I don't know if Barry will convert, but I know you planted seeds. So I had a well-learned man explain Yeshua as the long-awaited messiah, and you helped us test the reasoning behind Emma's name. We had hoped you would use both of our names when Emma was listening, and you did. You really helped the future of this program more than you know."

"I don't see how our conversations helped Emma."

"Several things happened. First, I repeated myself a few times. I already knew the answers, but I asked you about baptism or a works-based faith. I asked you about particular scriptures more than once."

Yes, he sure did.

"This not only elicited certain responses medically, but it forced Emma to evaluate how your responses raised or lowered your heart rate, your blood pressure, and your breathing."

"Ok, that part is amazing."

"But that was just part of it. Did you ever pick up on the fact that I never called Barry James, and he never called me James, except that one time at breakfast this morning?"

The more I thought about it, the more I realized James had used terms like "butler" or "someone" and never called his brother by his real name, nor by his alias. "I take it that was to test Emma's cognitive abilities?"

"Yes, correct. But more like it proved that she had cognitive abilities. Every day, we have a debrief with her about her activities. She immediately picked up on the switch and questioned what we were doing. We explained that we wanted to help her learn. She loves to learn. So she played along.

But we had to be careful never to use the correct names and also be careful never to use the fake names either."

"I must say that is a brilliant technique," I said in amazement.

"There is more. I truly believe that there is no doubt that when I leave this world, Barry will listen to our conversations and will maybe convert someday and not face his name being blotted out of the book of life."

"Was it his dream?"

"Oh, yes! I almost forgot to tell you about that. It's on the recording, too, but I will tell you. He did share that dream with me, but he was adamant that it not be used for Emma's learning. So, I had to write it all down. When you ripped it and lost part of it, I thought it was the end of our time together. So I took the secret elevator to your room when you were not in there."

I jumped up. "Excuse me, what?"

"Sit down, please. Each corner room has a secret stairwell, which you saw when you went to the wine cellar, and a secret elevator, too. This room has each as well. It goes to the third floor. Each night I came back to this room, it was not so I could lie in this uncomfortable bed. It was so I could take the elevator to the third floor. It's where my and Barry's suites are located."

"Amazing. You know, one night I thought I heard an elevator sound, but I didn't think much of it. Wow, James, the secrets of this house. I am blown away and not sure whether to be angry or amazed. I am a little of both, I guess."

"I really didn't like hiding things from you. You truly did help me a lot in my faith, and I know Emma has learned a lot from you."

"Well, that's good. Praise God. But how, how did you get all of these recordings? The mics must be extremely sensitive."

"Well, yes, they are highly sensitive, and they are numerous, too. Each room, save this one, has seventy tiny mics specifically for collecting health data. Then each room has a mic in the smoke detector for capturing voices."

"And all these tie in that system in the gym?"

"Oh, good, you found the gym. That was what I was hoping you would find when I told you to explore. Did you play basketball?"

"No, I didn't have time. But I did find…" I stopped myself. Gene's words played out in my mind. *Don't tell Mr. Goldberg.* "Umm, does Gene know about the switch?"

"The only two people who have been in this house that don't know are you and Bernice. She is the one you saw this morning. She comes in for Sunday breakfast so the chef can go to church. He's a Mormon, unfortunately. It didn't seem worth telling her. But you were saying you didn't play ball?"

Dodged that one. "No, I did not. I didn't know if I should have been in there, and I wanted to respect that." *Sounds like he doesn't know about the room, or he is avoiding it for some reason.* "So, you already knew Jesus before I came here, and you wanted me to both be part of your elaborate AI testing and to give you info for proselytizing your brother?"

"Jake, Emma tells me that my days are short. She has noticed a slowing of my breathing patterns and a lower heart rate. She believes my heart is failing, and my liver and kidneys as well. But I can't thank you enough for what you have done. Per my agreement with Barry, I will have to ask you to leave tomorrow. But I want you to do something."

"What is it? What can I do for you?"

"Please take a few minutes to watch the video on the iPad." I looked at the video, which now showed flowcharts with a heading 'The Path To AGI' across the top. "It's not the one that is playing now. It's the one labeled: 'Jake Watch'. Very clever name, huh?"

I let out a laugh. "Ok, should I watch it now?"

"If not sooner. I do hope you know how much I appreciate what you have done. And our agreement still stands. I will give…"

He stopped, and his eyes widened. He tried to speak, but no words came.

"What is it?"

He pointed to the door. "I heard a noise outside." He then pointed behind him and managed to say, "Behind the curtain. Go!"

I didn't think. I just ran. As I reached the curtain he apparently tried to tell me about, I walked through a small opening. I heard a muffled voice. I didn't stay to find out who it was. I saw a door along a wall. It was locked. I tried the key Jennifer gave me, and it surprisingly opened it. *Must be a master key.* A stairway went up and down. I took the down path, and when I opened the door, I recognized the narrow hallway. I was almost directly across from the gym. I took a moment to study the space patterns, trying to determine how I might have just taken steps. I didn't think long as I knew there would be a door at the end of the hall. I felt the temptation to try the key on the gym door, but ran past it. Once outside, I ran to the edge of the house, turned the corner, and spotted Jennifer waiting for me by the garage.

I ran closer. "We need to talk!"

"Yes, we do." Gene walked into view. "We have a lot to talk about."

I stopped dead in my tracks. I saw a leather case hanging around his neck. I didn't know the jurisdiction or affiliation, but Gene was not who he said he was. That seemed to be the modus operandi for everyone at this house. But I knew I would find out the truth soon.

Chapter Seventeen

Asp & Viper

My run narrowed to a slow walk. My mind raced faster than my feet as I approached the garage. Gene had proved to be as mysterious as the entire week. *He caught me in the room and didn't arrest me, but he said he was not a cop. Now, he is standing in front of me with a badge around his neck.* The leather wallet-sized case held by a silver chain hung squarely in the center of his chest. As I approached, I noticed that Jennifer was not handcuffed and that Gene was not holding a weapon against her. *Is he FBI?*

As I stood three feet before them, I didn't need to ask. He opened the leather case and revealed a picture on the right and a circular gold badge bearing the letters BIS. Around a circle with the famous eagle seal in the center, and also in blue were the words Bureau of Internal Security. Underneath, at the edge of the shield, I read "Special Agent." *Definitely federal, but not FBI.* My mind wandered, but Gene revealed himself.

"Gene Walters, special agent, Bureau of Internal Security, Department of Commerce."

"DOC, that explains everything. Are you investigating the Goldbergs for the AI sales?"

"I cannot comment on that, Jake. I am going to need both of you to come with me, please." he gently pushed Jennifer, but she resisted.

"Where are we going?" Jennifer demanded.

"I will explain soon, but we need to get to a safe place. Jake, do you have the iPad?"

"No." I had tucked it in my jeans behind my back.

"Sir, if you don't want to be charged with obstruction of justice, I suggest you hand over the evidence."

"I may be wrong, but BIS agents don't carry handcuffs. You are more of an investigator, are you not?"

"Yes, but within the hour, this place will be swarming with FBI, Homeland Security, and DEA agents! Trust me, you want to be seen cooperating with me when they arrive. If you have the device, I need it. I know he recorded a video for you on it."

"DEA and Homeland?" Curiosity piqued.

"Formality. DEA for the most likely legal pharmaceuticals on premise, and Homeland because of my investigation, and that is all I can say about that. Please, we need to go back inside. Follow me."

Gene didn't wait for an argument; he started walking, turned back briefly to see us both following, and then continued. We walked around the left side of the house to the door I had previously exited. He entered first and held the door open for us. He proceeded to the gym door, but not before putting his index finger to his mouth to counsel us to remain quiet. Neither of us felt a need to argue.

Once inside the gym, Gene shut the door behind us. We walked down the steps to the floor. Gene proceeded to the center court, where three metal chairs awaited us. *He planned for this.*

"Sit down, please." Gene glanced at his watch as he took the final chair. "We have about thirty-five to forty minutes. Let me talk. I will debrief the field agent, and that will avoid you being detained in handcuffs, but at this point, please consider yourselves detained by the FBI."

Jennifer gasped.

"It's okay. You did not do anything wrong. Trust me, if you had, I would not have warned you about what is coming. I appreciate what both of you have done. Jake, may I have that iPad now?"

"Just because you have a badge does not mean you are a real agent. We need to be careful. We don't know who is who right now." Jennifer showed a flash of wisdom as she looked my way.

"Okay. Hold on."

Gene reached for his phone, swiped a couple of times, and held it out so we could view the video now playing. I saw the President of the United States speaking in the White House Press Room. He stood at a podium, and to his right stood Gene. "I am honored to present the Special Recognition Award to special agent Gene Walters for his efforts in preventing a tragedy six months ago..." He pulled the phone back. "Need more evidence? And no, before you suggest it, it's not AI. I helped other agencies disrupt a terrorist plot. Being in the BIS, I don't have arrest powers, but I do have a phone, and my phone call to the FBI led to the arrest of a notorious terrorist. That was five years ago, long before I went undercover here."

"Okay, okay, but there is a video on it that James said I need to watch." I reached behind me and grabbed the iPad, handing it to Gene.

He received it and walked to the wall. Seconds later, we heard the sounds of Velcro being separated.

Jennifer turned and gasped. "What the heck?"

I didn't turn. I grabbed her hand. "Yeah, a house full of secrets."

"Did you know about that?"

"I found it accidentally one night, yes."

"What's in there?"

"It seems it was a monitoring office when this place had cameras."

"No one ever mentioned cameras at all."

"I don't think they are active anymore, and I bet I know why. I found that room because the wall mat had peeled back a little while I was in here. I went in, and Gene found me. I then overheard him talking to someone when I came back to get my phone. My guess now is that it was his handler. Anyway, cameras can give off subtle sounds, and I imagine they were removed so Emma could work better."

"Here he comes."

She was right. I looked up, and Gene walked back to us carrying the iPad. He grabbed his phone and dialed a number. I looked at Jennifer, and she at me.

"We got them. Confession by Viper." He waited for a reply. "Viper is in the hospital room, and Scarlett confirmed sedation of Asp." We waited. He began walking again and took his seat. "Forty and Scarlett are with me for debrief...Ok, I will confirm." He set the phone down. "Do we know if Barry is still sedated?"

"He should be. He should sleep for hours unless awakened with smelling salts."

Gene put the phone to his head again. "Confirmed, he will be in the library..."

"I don't think he is sleeping."

"Hold on." The phone went to his lap again. He looked me in the eye. "Explain, please."

I remembered the file I had viewed in the secret room. I looked across the floor as I processed the memory. *The file started with BG. I thought that was Barry, but it must have meant the one I knew as James. Gene must have had secret surveillance on top of Emma's*

"Jake, no time. Please explain."

"Umm, the one I knew of as James, but it's Barry. I think you called him "Asp." I think he came into the room just before I exited."

"Let me call you back, Agent Smith." I heard the beep as Gene looked at me. "You have about twenty seconds to explain."

"I was speaking with Bar...I mean, James, and he said he heard something outside. When I had gone into the room, I caught a glimpse of Barry," I said in a drawn-out tone, "sleeping in the library."

"Yes, Jennifer sedated him with some tea." He glanced at her. "And you gave him the dose we agreed upon?"

"Well, I am a nurse, and I am not a nurse anesthetist. But I have been around to know that for a man his age and with his approximate height and weight, that seemed a bit much, so I halved the dose."

I jumped at the noise. Jennifer started crying. Gene had slammed his foot down on the gym floor, causing an echo to reverberate for several seconds.

"We agreed on the procedure. I trusted you. What did you do with the other half?"

"I flushed it down Jake's sink. In his room." That explained why she ran the water.

"Jennifer, this is a problem. If he awakes and escapes before the FBI arrives, you will be arrested for obstruction of justice."

"Jake?"

I slid my chair across the gym floor, so I sat directly next to her, and put my hand on her back to comfort her. She leaned in and hugged me.

"I don't want to go to jail, but I felt it would harm him. That was a large dose."

"Wait!" Gene grabbed the tablet from his lap and scrolled a few times. The sound recording began to play. His finger moved the slider near the end. I heard my voice. "So, should I watch it now?" James' voice came in after mine. "If not sooner..."

"What on earth? How did you..."

"Shhh!" Gene spat as he yelled at me.

I heard pounding and a curtain swish. Then a voice. "Hello, brother. How are you doing today? Any..." The voice clearly belonged to Barry, whom I once believed to be named James.

"That's definitely Asp. He's awake."

"Asp?" I asked. "I assume Barry is Asp, James is Viper, and that would make Jennifer Scarlett and me forty?"

Gene didn't answer. He pressed a button on his phone. "Asp is alert. I repeat, Asp is alert. Next steps?" I looked at Jennifer and mouthed *Forty?*

"Your book."

I realized how my code name had been given. Forty represented my book. It tied the name to me but kept my identity hidden from anyone who might have been listening in. Gene continued talking on the phone as I looked down at the iPad and realized what had happened. I looked at Jennifer. "Did you know?"

"I'm sorry, Jake. I didn't know he was an agent. I knew the iPad would record everything, though, but I thought he was setting up Barry."

"Well, clearly he was. I mean, I am not mad. But I wish you had just told me."

"She worked on orders, Jake. She did well." I had not noticed Gene had ended his phone call. "The FBI is closer than we realized. We need to stay in this gym and only open the door when the code word is given."

"And that code word is?" I asked.

"Open this door immediately!" the shout came from the other side. "You stole my key from me. I have already called the police." It was the butler's voice.

"Yeah, that's not the code word," Gene added with a smile.

"Are we safe?" Jennifer asked with a shattered voice.

"We are fine. He won't get in." Gene replied.

"Mr. Anderson, your bags will be shipped to you. I must ask that you leave the premises immediately." The voice of who I knew as James but now know as Barry echoed through the gym.

"Jake, I have all I need off this now. You can watch the video. In fact, stay in here, both of you, until I come get you." Gene swiftly moved to the door. Once there, he pulled out a pen, which I assumed had a built-in microphone. "Mr. Goldberg, it's Gene. I can't open the door because it's barricaded. It will take me a few minutes to get through this. Sir, I think Jake believes the Emma code drives are in the secret room. He's in there now trying to find them."

"What an idiot! The drives with the code are all secured under the garage floor." He sighed deeply. "I hope he hasn't told my brother about the room. I figured he found the gym and the room on Sabbath. There was a half-hour when Emma did not detect his presence, and I know he was not with James. He must have seen that day as a perfect opportunity to explore." There was another sigh. "Wait, how did you know about the…Who on earth are you? What? No, I will not. Stop pointing that thing at me. No, I will not get on the ground."

Gene returned, "Pretty sure not only is the FBI here, but I heard crackling. I think Barry got tazed, and I got the proof I had been looking for. I guess that Jake, your car has been sitting all week on top of the stockpile of encrypted hard drives with Emma on them. I never thought to look in the oil-change pit. Smart man, that Barry Goldberg." He clapped his hands together. "Well, it's in the hands of the FBI now. They will be…"

"Freeze, on the ground!"

"Here any minute." Gene turned and flashed his badge. "Special Agent Walters, BIS."

"Stand down, special agent. That is my guy." I didn't recognize the voice. "Everyone is secured, Agent Walters. It's over."

"Thanks. Jake, Jennifer, this is Special Agent In Charge, Trey Smith."

Agent Smith entered the room as the FBI agent walked out. I saw Barry, handcuffed, being led away in the distance. I turned my gaze to Agent Smith, who gave me a big smile. "Nice to meet you again, Mr. Anderson."

"You!" I couldn't think of any other words. I had met Agent Smith briefly in the driveway the previous day while I was walking. He had been outside the gate talking to someone, probably Gene, before a black Escalade picked him up.

"Yes, Jake, he is the one you saw. Ruined our weekly debrief with your unplanned walk," he smiled as he walked toward the door. You two stay here for right now until I brief the agent in charge."

"Umm, Gene, I mean Special Agent Walters."

"Yes, Jake."

"Can I possibly go up and see James. I am sure you didn't handcuff him."

"No, Jake. We need to secure the area first. I will be sure you get a chance to see him before you leave. If all proves true, I don't believe he will be arrested as part of this investigation. He kept his nose clean. Now, whether it was or not, I don't know, but we have nothing on him. Even the video he made for you didn't implicate him. He started to walk back. "By the way, you can watch that. It's ready to go when you are. Definitely watch it. I will return within the hour."

I picked up the tablet, found the video, and started watching. Much of it read like a verbatim account of what we discussed in his room. But when we thought it would end, he asked someone to leave the room. "This is for Jake only." He remained silent before the camera. In the distance, a door shut.

Chapter Eighteen

All Secrets Revealed

I sat with great anticipation. The video ran 25 minutes, and I estimated my talk with James lasted about 15 minutes. Much of what he said in the first twelve minutes matched what he told me; however, in the video on the iPad Jennifer had given me, he never mentioned anything his brother, Barry, had done illegally.

When I first met the family, James asked if I knew who he was, and I said I assumed he was Barry Goldberg. That was my first test. If I had failed that and recognized Barry, who was impersonating James, and disguised as the butler, as Barry Goldberg, the charade would have ended. The website Jennifer sent me to research Barry was a fake, and I never thought to look deeper into his background. I fell for the trap and was used by the brothers. The sting wore off when I heard what James said about our discussions.

In the video, James asked someone to leave the room. When this part came, Jennifer reached across me and paused the video. "Do you want me to leave?"

"No, not at all. I am sure what is being said will be fine for you to hear."

I played the video, and once again, James spoke.

"Jake, I can't thank you enough. I have already arranged for the payment to be made as agreed. Well, I agreed upon. I know you did not want to be paid for your work here, but I insisted. Please tell Jennifer as well that she has been properly compensated already."

"Well, I thought it would be fun to be my brother for a week, but I know now that I never want to be my brother. You don't know this, but we would have conversations after hours, when everyone was asleep. We would discuss and debate everything you had spoken about throughout the day. By the fifth day, he realized I had already converted. I tried to reason with him about many of the things you mentioned. As I am sure I told you when we met." He paused and thought for a moment. "Wait, we haven't met yet." He laughed, and I did too. "But I know we are going to meet soon, and I will tell you that you taught me things I had never heard. You are extremely gifted by our great creator and savior. In particular, when you showed me how many people patterned themselves after Jesus. Abraham and the almost sacrifice of Isaac, Moses and speaking to the rock, as a spiritual matter, rather than striking it, as a physical matter, and comparing the crossing of the Red Sea to that of being born of water and the entering into the promised land as being born of the Spirit. Then there was David, whom I knew Messiah would come from, but you tied the pieces of Saul's rejection as king to the rejection of God's ways by tradition. It made so much sense. I don't feel I have time to cover even Joshua, Elijah, and blessed Jeremiah. You did well explaining the messiah from the Tanakh."

"But then you also covered some of the New Testament. How amazing to behold that the Father and the Son worked together to establish a New Covenant for His people, and the Gentiles, too. I always thought Jeremiah 31 was for my people, and yes, it is. But who are the children of Abraham? Not just by blood, but by those who believe and have faith. God has established a covenant by blood, but not the blood of bulls and rams, but by the blood of His son, Jesus. Hebrews 8 and 10 make this so clear, and now I see it better. I tried to reason this with Barry, but he would not listen."

"I admit one more lie I told you. I had only read scattered parts of the New Testament until last night. I read Romans, and it helped so much. When I finished, I went back and read Acts. The day of Shavuot, or as you would call it Pentecost, wow. Amazing what the Spirit of God did. I only wish I had more time to ask you why so many Christians make doctrines out of that one chapter in that one book. I believe it is essential, but I see this group going a bit far with their interpretations at times. I feel that, in many ways, all denominations of the Christian Church do this. "

"Jake, let me say that if I had more time on this earth, I would probably ask you why anyone feels they need to add to the amazing sacrifice of my ancestor in blood and faith, Jesus of Nazareth. I read how some denominations feel that baptism is required as part of salvation. But even Paul writes in his letter to the Corinthians. 'For Christ did not send me to baptize, but to preach the gospel—not with wisdom and eloquence, lest the cross of Christ be emptied of its power.' That alone tells me that it is not required, or he would have baptized a lot more people. Besides, adding such a burden is what my people have done for centuries. We don't eat cheeseburgers for fear of mixing milk and meat, as it is the same as boiling a young goat in its mother's milk. Oh, the obscenity of such a burden. I now know that Jesus meant what He said when He spoke to Nicodemus. He said we are saved by our belief in Him alone. I know we touched on this in one conversation, but I took it further. Thank you for your words. "

"Sure, I think all should celebrate the baptism, as John pronounced my brethren when he was questioned in the wilderness, but denied being Elijah, the Prophet, or the messiah. John told them that someone was already there, and they didn't see him. Blinded by tradition, they were, but even now, churches are blinded by other traditions."

"Which brings me to, you are a pastor, Jake, but you are not a traditional pastor. You were called by God to be a pastor, but not in the way the traditional Christian church has defined it. Wow, God bless you, Jake, for being obedient to The Word."

He coughed a few times and continued. "Jake, I wish I could go on. Perhaps you can write a book about our encounter. I am certain it would sell well. In case you do, could I ask that you share all we discussed with others and encourage them to read the Bible, all of it, for themselves? But also Jake, encourage them to seek God in understanding it. They will have lives greatly enhanced if they seek a relationship with our God and live with Him daily. My life has changed dramatically since He allowed me to see His truth. Teach them, Jake, let none of them escape God's loving embrace. I praise God for giving us His Son and saving us from our sins, but even more, I praise God for the chance to know Him in this life, and I am very excited for the next. Make sure they know Him in this life. Don't just look forward to heaven. Teach them to live with God today. It's worth it. So worth it."

"I am glad to have met you. Thank you for visiting us, and remember, Emma is always listening. You talk in your sleep. I am not sure what is happening with you and Charlotte, but I do hope you reconcile with her. I bless you now in the name of Jesus Christ, our Lord, who calls us, persuades us, and does not force us to love Him and know Him. What a great freedom. God bless you, Jake."

I wiped the tears from my eyes before setting the tablet on the ground. Jennifer had stood and looked away. But she listened.

"You're a great man, Jake Anderson."

"We serve a great God, Jennifer. He loves you and loves James too."

"Loved."

I look in the direction of the voice. Gene had walked back in. "Can you two join me outside? It's standard protocol that you be checked medically, and then the FBI will probably have some questions and instructions for you."

I had a sinking feeling. Gene had said 'loved.' *Did James pass?* I reached the bottom of the steps, looked up, and said, "Passed?"

"Yes, Jake. I am sorry to say that James Goldberg has passed away."

"I knew it would not be long, but I thought maybe a few more days or even a week."

"Yeah, we all thought that, Jennifer, but I went in to tell him that we had arrested his brother, and he didn't respond. One of our doctors on scene confirmed it and called the death. He's in heaven now."

"Indeed, he is. He believed all along. I am grateful to have helped him, and I wish Barry had come around, too. But sometimes religion gets so embedded in a person that pride won't let the Lord change their minds. Sometimes traditions are so powerful in a person's heart that they become hardened. All we can do now is honor James' request and try to convince as many people as we can that Jesus is the Messiah."

"Agreed. But I need to get you checked out. Let's go."

Jennifer stepped before me, and together we walked up the steps. I wanted to go to the room above us and see James one more time, but I also didn't want to get arrested. We proceeded outside, and the agents were already swarming the garage like angry yellow jackets. One by one, the blue-jacketed men and women carried black boxes, presumably containing hard drives, to an awaiting black van. The DEA grabbed Jennifer for questioning.

I heard a voice behind me that I recognized. He called my name, and I turned to see Shane standing before me. I waited for him to get closer. "Charlotte?"

"Not now, Jake. We have to get through this debrief, but when I heard you were here, I wanted to come to you, and the lead agent permitted me. I need to know all you know about this AI program. Let's go over here," he pointed in the direction of an even larger black van. It resembled a large U-HAUL, but was painted black and had an FBI logo on the side.

***

An hour after we entered the van, Shane pulled me aside away from all other prying ears. He spoke as we continued to walk down the winding driveway, "You played a huge part in this. I hope you know that."

"I give credit to James. I believe he sincerely wanted Emma to be used for good, but also knew his brother had other plans. I never asked him, but I wonder if he knew of Gene's cover. Do you know?"

"I have not spoken with Agent Walters yet, but I am sure that will come out in the investigation. Regardless, it seems that James didn't want his brother to sell it to a foreign organization. James seemed like a good man."

"I agree. You can't know a person fully after a week, but I feel I know him a lot more. He is a good man with a good heart, but I can't say the same for Barry. He was not a fan of me."

"No doubt about it. He kept bashing you and blaming you. He insisted you were the undercover agent."

"Does he know it was Gene?"

"No, and he never will." he stopped walking, and I did as well. He turned and breathed a deep sigh. "Now, about Charlotte. I'm afraid I don't have good news."

I took a deep breath. I turned around and took a few steps away from him before returning. I felt tears well up in my eyes. "Dead?"

Chapter Nineteen

Cove Fort

There I stood in the entryway of the square stone fort with three trees growing in the sandy courtyard within. I had been there four years earlier when a small dog chased me back to my car. My whole life changed when Timmy and Jane died in that car accident. It changed even more when I went to a church and defended a nineteen-year-old girl against an arrogant, self-centered, ego-maniac pastor who believed he heard from God to build a church. My life changed again when I met that purple-haired girl at the airport in Indianapolis and brought her home to live with me. I was her 'Dad,' and she was my adopted 'daughter'.

I replayed my final conversation with her. It hurt, but it also felt cathartic. I drove her to the airport early one morning. I believed I would see her again some day, but now I am not sure.

"Jake, I have to confess something before we depart."

I swallowed hard and prayed silently. The past week had been tenuous at best. "What is it?"

"I don't really want to say this but it's true and how it started at the beginning is not how it ended up and I want you to know that I did enjoy our time together."

I couldn't imagine what she meant. "Go on."

"I saw you as a way out at first. I mean, I was lost and my mom had died and I didn't have a job and well I felt lost. I saw you as an escape. Sure, I wanted a dad, but I also needed a place to live and really thought I would start a new life with you."

"I knew that." It hurt, but I knew it. I felt compassion for her situation and wanted to provide for her, but I knew she used me.

"I wanted to get that off my chest. I mean, I did enjoy getting to know you and in some way, you will always be my dad, but I really need to get to know my uncle for who he really is."

"It sounds like you are saying goodbye for good, Charlotte."

She sighed deeply. "No, it's not that. I will be back. You can come to Colorado. We can visit somewhere in the middle again sometime."

"But you think you will be gone for a while?"

"I don't know what I am doing. I just don't know." She turned her body toward the window and that was the last we spoke until I parked at the airport. We didn't say much before she boarded, but she did give me a hug and whispered 'See you again some day.' before she scanned her ticket and boarded.

"Well, I have come full circle," I said aloud, knowing the four people visiting the American historical park didn't hear me, and if they did, wouldn't have any idea what I was talking about. *Full circle. What's next?* I looked up, half expecting God to split open the blue sky and drop me a note full of wisdom and direction. I knew, however, that it would not happen. My rental car was due back in Grand Junction by the end of the day, and if I left now, I would make it in plenty of time to catch a flight to Dallas and then fly back to Baltimore the next day.

But another option remained: drive to Davidson Ford, buy a small car, and travel along Interstate 70 again. *I don't think I will take forty days this time.* I stepped out and walked the perimeter of the fort. In the back of my mind, I hoped I would see a small beagle. I wanted something familiar to tell me it was not just a dream. Life is complex and constantly changing. I wanted something familiar to take my mind off what I heard.

But you still don't know for sure.

I didn't know. When I asked Shane if Charlotte was dead, he answered, 'I don't know.' When he landed in Cedar City, he had a voicemail from the search team's captain, looking for Charlotte. A hiker had found the body of a female in her twenties with brown hair and approximately Charlotte's height. Jane Doe had no identification and only the clothing on her back. He hoped Shane could provide an identification, but he had to handle the field mission in Cedar City. I glanced at my watch: Monday, four in the afternoon. Shane was at the hospital by now. I figured it would be only a matter of minutes before he called. *Then I will know.*

Once again, I played different scenarios in my mind. Maybe she moved to California. She had spoken of it many times. Maybe Julia convinced her to visit Ohio to see the new baby. Perhaps she moved to Canada to escape what she often called the 'daily grind of America, not a dream. ' That one always made me laugh.

My mind shifted again to Jennifer. Jane's sister left earlier in the day as I did. I dropped her off at the Cedar City airport, where she caught a flight to Honolulu for her next assignment as a traveling nurse. The entire drive consisted of her apologizing to me for lying about Barry and James.

"I really believed they intended to do good with Emma." She repeated several times.

I agreed that James' intentions remained solid. But Barry had made a lot of money in his life, and when his career dried up, he wanted more than investments to live on. I did have a chance to talk with Gene before I left, and he believed Barry would face federal civil charges for the private sale to a foreign party, but he could not comment on any criminal charges. As I grabbed my parting meal, the chef surfaced and introduced himself as Barry and James's cousin's son. He said James had no children and had never been married. Bessie was married to Barry, and Barry's son, Jacob, had not been seen for years. He said James would be flown back to New York, where he had been born, and buried in a local Jewish cemetery. No service, just the burial. I felt sorrow for him, but I knew also that I would see him in heaven someday, so I had comfort in the thought.

I will also see Charlotte, regardless of whether the body found proves to be hers or not. Wherever you are, Charlotte, I pray you are safe and happy, and if you have passed, I pray you are enjoying paradise.

I reached the arch leading to the courtyard again as my phone rang. It was Shane. I wasn't ready to hear, but I wanted to hear. The agony built up as the phone buzzed for the third time. I had to answer.

"Hello."

THE END

AFTERWORD

AI is here, and it is here to stay. Just as many revolutions have shaped our lives (Industrial, Television, Computer, Internet), the AI breakthrough, unlike a revolution, is shaping up to be one of those times we will someday look back on, and history books will teach students about for years to come. At the time of this writing, AI is still narrow. That means it is trained on large amounts of data and cannot escape that domain. This amount of data could be as large as a major search engine's or as small as a company's internal knowledge base. But AI remains narrow. That's a very good thing, and it's not really something to fear. The AI in Hollywood movies is known as Artificial General Intelligence, or AGI. In this book, Emma is a fictionalized depiction of what an AGI might look like. Imagine a computer as intelligent as a human, able to learn on its own, apply logic without code, and gain knowledge without being fed a large set of data. But also have no emotion, empathy, or mental awareness that God put in us to make us unique and separate. Basically, imagine a human without a soul. That's what AGI is theorized to be.

Many scientists say AGI is only a theory and will never be possible. But then again, Einstein said relativity was a theory, and today it has been proven to be a law. Will AGI come about? I don't know. But I do wonder whether some passages in the Bible hint at such a presence in this world. A computer that could, if possible, deceive even the elect of God. At the time of this writing, AGI systems like Emma are 100 percent impossible due to physical computing limitations. Some experts suggest quantum computers could allow AGI, but quantum computers are still unstable in many ways. But then again, the IBM PC was unstable on August 12, 1981 when it first released. But in late 2025, AGI is only theory and I suspect still a long way off. Now if you ask someone in the Silicon Valley or Bay Area in California where AI research is centered for the most part, they may say 2-3 years.

Beyond AGI is a theory of ASI (Artificial Super Intelligence) that goes beyond human intelligence. That's more science fiction, and that is where it will likely forever remain. But AGI, like Emma, who locked Jake in his room and learned how to tell when someone chose a different identity, it's a theory, but let's pray it never becomes a reality.

So, until we actually see it and see the effects, we are left with narrow AIs like ChatGPT, Siri, Alexa, Gemini and more. These are powerful tools and Emma being used for medical purposes is not far fetched at all and well within the realm of a narrow AI program. Afterall, sound waves are data and AI lives on data.

The best advice I can give for anyone who is fearful of AI, is pray. For anyone that wants to see AI succeed and scale to larger heights, I say pray. For anyone who is just learning what AI is, I say pray. Bottom line is pray. There truly is nothing in this world that will ever be greater than the one who created the world and redeemed us through his Son's sacrifice on an old rugged cross. If you don't have a strong relationship with God, seek Him out. He will be found. For you will find Him when you seek Him with your whole heart. (Jeremiah 29:13)

God Bless

OTHER WORKS

Forty On 70 – A Journey Of Faith And Healing. A desire for a bag of roasted peanuts changed Jake Anderson's life forever. Now, with the tragedy behind him and healing in the wings, Jake follows God's lead unusually. He believes he has heard God say to travel forty days on Interstate 70. Jake will do anything to be healed from his tragedy, so he sets out on a forty-day journey across the United States, traveling Interstate 70 from Utah to Maryland. Along the way, he encounters people, trials, and temptations, just to give up and return home early. Whom will he meet? Will he find healing? Join Jake on this incredible journey of faith and healing as he travels Forty on 70.

Four Hearts. She is all alone in the world, and fear has gripped her soul. She will do anything to find the father she always longed for and the one she never knew. A chance encounter at a church changes her course and direction, but will her deception be enough to start the new life she desires?

Unraveled, Charlotte's world is turned upside down when a mysterious phone call reveals a tantalizing clue about her past—someone claims to know the identity of her biological father. With her devoted dad, Jake, by her side, they embark on a journey to Columbus, Ohio, to uncover the truth. As they navigate the twists and turns of this emotional quest, Charlotte grapples with the possibility of an upheaval in her identity. Will she find the closure she seeks, or will the revelations shatter her sense of self beyond repair? As they travel through Ohio, it becomes clear that not everything is as it seems. Will their emotional vacation have a happy ending, or will her past finally reveal itself to be a series of lies and deceit?

COMING SOON

House Of Cards

Millridge, Ohio has always been easy to miss—a quiet town with one stoplight, one church, and a way of believing that what they have is enough. For Pastor Jared Wagner, Millridge Community Church is more than a calling. It's a place where names matter, where faith is practiced quietly, and where two hundred people gather each Sunday not because they must, but because they choose to.

When the city announces plans to seize their land for a massive new robotics facility operated by Helios Robotics Group, Millridge Community Church stands in the way—literally. What begins as a zoning dispute quickly becomes something far more personal: a battle between progress and presence, ambition and belonging.

As pressure mounts from city officials, developers, and even members of his own congregation, Jared must decide what it means to stand firm without becoming hard, to lead without conquering, and to resist pride disguised as righteousness. In a town about to disappear, House Of Cards asks a simple but unsettling question:

What is worth saving when the world tells you to move on?